AVENGER

DOMS OF MOUNTAIN BEND

BOOK 2

BJ Wane

Editors:
Kate Richards & Nanette Sipes

Cover Design & Formatting:
Joe Dugdale (sylv.net)

PUBLISHED BY BLUE DAHLIA

DISCLAIMER

This contemporary romantic suspense contains adult themes such as power exchange and sexual scenes. Please do not read if these offend you.

CONTENTS

PROLOGUE

Houston

❝This won't take long, Trey." Constance opened the back door of the Bentley, vibrating with anger and frustration.

"No problem, ma'am. I'll wait right here for you."

Reaching over the seat, she gave her loyal driver/bodyguard's shoulder a squeeze. What would she do without Trey's support? "Thanks. I just need to set this person straight on a few things."

"Anything I can do to help?"

He was always ready to jump to her defense, a loyal employee and companion. If she dared to risk her marriage with an affair, she would thank him by letting him appease the lust she often saw in his gaze as he looked at her, but there was no way she could get away with a tryst, especially one right under her husband, Blake's watchful eyes.

"I appreciate the offer, but I can handle her. Be right back."

She slid her legs out of the car and stood,

casting a look of disdain at the neighborhood diner, a run-of-the-mill place she normally wouldn't be caught dead frequenting. The audacity of *that woman* contacting her again after she'd turned her away once was almost too much to bear. It had taken Constance years of sacrifice and careful planning to finally achieve her goal of marrying for enough money to get anything she could ever want, and now this woman's resurrection of her past threatened everything.

After Rose Flynn had contacted her, revealing her knowledge that Constance was her adopted daughter's birth mother, she had looked her up and now recognized her seated at a booth even before Rose waved her over. Prepared to give her a larger piece of her mind this time, Constance schooled her expression into a haughty sneer as she strode across the stained linoleum floor.

Rose's face changed from hopeful to crestfallen by the time Constance reached the booth.

"How dare you contact me again after I specifically told your lawyer no." Her voice shook with fury at the woman's gall. Wasn't it bad enough she'd managed to uncover the truth after she'd taken so many precautions to erase any connection between her and the result of making the biggest mistake of her life?

"Please." Rose gestured to the other side of the table, the wobble in her voice leaving Constance unmoved. "If you could just hear me out, let me tell you about Poppy."

Constance's tone cut as sharp as her hand slicing through the air. "I have no interest in hearing about *your* daughter's woes, and I'm not about to risk my thirty-year marriage on a mistake I made when I was barely eighteen."

Translation – she wasn't about to risk the wealthy, elite status she'd enjoyed since marrying into one of Houston's richest families, not even for the child she'd given birth to thirty-two years ago.

"Then, just tell me who her father was. Maybe he has other children who are willing to help."

Her heart constricted, surprising Constance with the quick stab of pain after all these years. She might have started her pursuit of Michael Connelly for altruistic gain after having been raised in poverty, but she'd made the terrible mistake of letting herself fall for him and his lies. He'd waited until she was too far along in her pregnancy to get an abortion before dumping her, revealing he was an even colder bastard than she was a conniving bitch.

"Don't bother. He never wanted a child, so

I doubt he made that mistake twice. If you even attempt to contact me again, for any reason, you'll hear from my lawyer, and he'll eat yours for lunch. Are we clear?"

"Yes, on that point, but I'll never understand how people like you can live with yourselves, how you can even sleep at night."

Constance placed her hand on the scarred tabletop, her ring finger adorned with a large, gaudy diamond that glittered under the fluorescent lighting. She curled her sculpted lips and drawled, "After I indulge in a glass of Chateau Lafite Rothschild and slip between my silk designer sheets, trust me, I have no problem. I can see you think I'm a royal bitch, and you're correct. Contact me again, and I'll show you just what a bitch I can be, starting with a lawsuit for libel. I don't think your husband's meager teacher's pension could handle that, do you?"

"We won't give up trying to help our daughter. We found you; we'll find him."

Constance didn't understand the determined glint in the other woman's eyes or her firm voice. Then again, she'd only cared about one person in her life, and he left her brokenhearted, nine months pregnant with his child, and she'd taken care never to let anyone matter again.

Confident Rose wouldn't try, or succeed if she did, Constance replied, "Knock yourself out, just don't involve me." She straightened, pivoted on her Vuitton heels, and strode out with her head held at a high, regal angle.

Trey was standing on the curb, holding the door open for her when she exited the diner. She gave him a beaming smile and patted his broad chest, the rapid beat of his heart under her hand making her blood pump with satisfaction. "All taken care of. Come on. I'll treat you to a nightcap on the way home."

His eyes slid toward the diner window then back at Constance. "If you're sure there's nothing I can do to help, then I'd like that."

"I'm sure."

She didn't know what he meant by helping, but she suspected, as an ex-Marine, he was talking about more of a physical threat than her verbal ones. She wouldn't hesitate to use everything within her financial power to bring down the Flynns if they continued to come to her for help in providing a suitable bone-marrow transplant for their daughter. Strangely enough, given her lack of conscience toward the ailing child she'd born, she drew the line at causing either of them physical harm, even if she did enjoy Trey's devotion and his willingness to come to her defense. Just because her prenuptial agreement kept her from indulging in a crass affair with the hired help didn't mean she couldn't relish the lust and overprotectiveness her driver and bodyguard didn't bother hiding from her.

Sliding into the luxury car, Constance settled on the leather seat, hoping this was the end to the Flynns' pursuit of her DNA.

Rose Flynn watched the elegant woman who had given birth to her beloved daughter walk out of the diner with the same look of disdain she'd worn when entering. Despite the fancy coiffured sweep of her blonde hair that was nothing like Poppy's fiery curls, she had seen the resemblance in the woman's bright-blue eyes, small, straight nose, full lips, and tall, slender build. Poppy's lanky body was still recovering from the bouts of chemotherapy her diagnosis of Hodgkin's lymphoma had required, but her girl never let anything keep her down for long.

A tightness clenched around Rose's heart as she thought of the pain and illness Poppy had suffered these past months, and the one rejection of new bone marrow from a donor needed to replace stem cells destroyed by the harsh treatments. The donor cells would have also helped find and kill future cancer cells, something she would have to watch for the rest of her life. The daughter of her heart had been a delightful handful to raise, smart as a whip, constantly flitting from one thing to another, barely taking a breath in between, sometimes without thinking it through. Rose and her husband, Steve, adored her, would do anything for her, including contacting this cold woman to beg for her help.

Rose fought back tears. How could her Poppy have come from anyone that callous and coldhearted? The thought of losing her daughter hurt so much, she was tempted to try blackmail, threaten to go to Constance Mayfield's husband and risk jail, anything to ensure Poppy lived a long, healthy life. But all that would accomplish was a brief sense of satisfaction from bringing the heartless woman down, since no one could force her to become a donor.

Beth, Rose's friend and owner of the diner walked up. "What a bitch." Reaching over, she squeezed Rose's shoulder. "Don't worry, hon. Poppy is young, and cancer-free right now, and that woman will get what's coming to her someday."

Rose looked around the crowded diner, noting the sympathetic glances from friends in the neighborhood who knew Poppy, and recalling the angry glares they leveled on Constance Mayfield's back as she walked out. Tidbits of the woman's visit to the diner would seep out and make the circles, and that would have to suffice for payback.

"I doubt it. Those types rarely do. As long as there's always a likelihood of the cancer returning, I won't rest easy until she has a successful transplant." She fretted just as much over what her unpredictable daughter would do now she'd been told the odds of another nonfamilial donation ending any different than the first one weren't in her favor. At least the staff at MD Anderson refused to give up, which helped.

"But time's on her side, so let's think positive."

"That's what her doctors told her and us. Thanks, Beth." She gave her friend a look of gratitude then sipped her iced tea.

"That's what friends are for, hon. Are you going to tell her about this meeting?"

Rose nodded, sighing. "I won't keep it a secret from her. She won't like it, but she'll understand."

"She's a good girl. Give me a minute, and I'll box up Steve's cherry pie and add a piece of Poppy's favorite."

"Yes, she's the best," Rose whispered as Beth went to get the desserts. She wouldn't give up her search for a suitable donor, regardless of yet another disappointment.

****

"You didn't. Please tell me you didn't." As soon as Poppy opened her front door and saw her mother's face, she knew what she'd done. Standing back, she beckoned her inside. "Come in then tell me."

Rose entered Poppy's apartment with slumped shoulders, handing her a small plastic bag from Beth's Place on the corner of her parents' block. She'd grown up walking down to the diner to hook up with friends for a burger and loved Beth's homemade cooking. "Is this supposed to appease me?" She held up the bag.

"It's chocolate pecan."

"You do know how to get to me." She held her breath as Rose walked into the living area and her gaze zeroed in on the suitcases. "Don't be upset, Mom."

"Eat your pie and tell me your plans," Rose returned, her voice resigned.

This was one of those rare times Poppy felt guilty about her constant desire for change, to explore something new after she'd gotten too comfortable with her current job, or relationship, or just the day-to-day routine. Hence, three degrees and two certifications, five relationships that never went further than a few months of dating, and an often-depleted bank account from taking a trip as soon as she made enough money to afford where she wanted to go next. Heck, she even ended up getting bored with sex after the first few nights burning up the sheets.

Grabbing a fork in the kitchen, she padded over to the sofa and took a seat next to her mother, who, at sixty-eight, was showing the strains Poppy's health had put her through. She gently patted her hand. "Mom, I'm fine, no cancer right now. I may as well enjoy what I can while I'm feeling good. Who knows, I may be one of the lucky few who doesn't relapse."

"You need those stem cells, even without the cancer."

"And she refused, again. After learning she must have paid someone to put a deceased woman's name on my birth certificate, you shouldn't be surprised. I'm still irked you and Dad spent so much money finding that out."

"I'd say we're lucky a nurse who was working in that rural hospital was still there and was an avid follower of the rich and elite, but having her recognize Mrs. Mayfield all those years ago from newspaper wedding photos turned out to be a godsend."

"Quit beating yourself up over her rejection. I'm willing to try another donor when they get a possible match." She opened the Styrofoam box and almost drooled at the decadent slice of creamy dark-chocolate pie topped with nuts. "Share this with me."

"No, you need the calories, not me."

Poppy shot her mother a quick grin. "Hey, don't you know the skinny, anorexic look is in?"

In a spontaneous move so like her, Rose reached over and hugged Poppy really quickly then released her, sitting back to point at the pie. "Eat and tell me where you're off to this time."

Shoveling in a large forkful, she hummed in pleasure of the creamy concoction and swallowed before answering. "Idaho. It should be nice going north this time of year, and I got a gig managing a sheep ranch."

Shaking her head, Rose's smile turned rueful. "Only you would jump from corporate management to tending sheep on some farm."

"Hey, it's about time I used my degree in animal husbandry, and it's a ranch, not a farm, or so I was told by Old Man Sanders, my new boss. God, this is good." She released a throaty moan as she took the last bite.

"Glad you like it. Please tell me you're not going to call him that to his face."

Standing, she picked up the empty box and carried it to the trash in the kitchen, saying over her shoulder, "It's how he referred to himself and informed me that's what everyone calls him. My last day at the bank is Friday, and I plan on leaving Saturday morning. How about if I take you and Dad out for dinner?"

"We'd like that."

Poppy padded over to Rose and walked her to the door where she gave Poppy a kiss on the cheek. Another twinge of guilt tightened her abdominal muscles as her mother tried to keep her face averted enough to hide the sadness and worry her health, and now this trip, caused Rose. Poppy couldn't help who she was, and her parents had never tried to suppress or discourage her need for constant change.

Laying a hand on her mother's arm as she opened the door, Poppy sought to put her mind at ease by reminding Rose of her flighty nature. "I'll get tired of smelly sheep and this craggy boss before you know it, just like the other flash-in-the-pan jobs I took for a break from the tedium. And I always call every day."

"I don't bother telling you not to because I love it, and you. See you Friday. I want to go to Da Marco's."

"Of course you do." The fancy Italian restaurant was one of Houston's most popular, and most expensive. "I'll make reservations."

Closing the door, Poppy surveyed her half-filled suitcases and thought of all she still needed to do between now and Friday. The busy schedule would help keep her mind off her parents' worry and the despair the wicked witch had caused her mother. She'd never been curious about her birth mother, not even after she'd gotten sick. Rose was the one who insisted they seek a court order to open the sealed adoption records, citing urgent, exigent circumstances. Tom Broman, their family lawyer and friend for as long as Poppy could remember, had come through for them, finding a sympathetic judge and producing the name Cassandra Jacobs as her birth mother. It had taken a considerable amount of money toward further investigating to discover the lengths to which the woman had gone to keep her identity a secret.

To say Constance Mayfield was displeased when Tom contacted her and told her the situation was an understatement. When Poppy heard the woman had threatened her parents with a massive lawsuit, she'd put her foot down and insisted they let it go. Her father had agreed, the worry on his lined face evident. She thought her mother had accepted that dead end but apparently not.

Now that she knew her birth mother's identity, she wanted even less to do with her than before, which she never thought possible. She found the very idea she carried the same DNA as that money-grubbing, greedy bitch abhorrent. Rose and Steve exuded the true meaning of parenthood, and parental love, and Poppy would never accept any overtures from the vessel who had born her. It would have been hard enough to willingly accept more of her DNA, but she figured she could suck up that much if it meant saving her life. Maybe.

Tabling any further thoughts on her health, or possible future health issues, she put off doing more packing to dig through her college textbooks and brush up on the chapters dealing with sheep raising and care.

****

Idaho

"Damn it, Mom, why are you seeing him again? Your face hasn't healed from last week."

Dakota glared at his mother, clenching his hands to keep from plowing his fist into the thin wall of their cheap apartment in frustration and anger. He didn't care about anyone except his mother, and it was bad enough watching how hard she toiled cleaning people's houses, but he couldn't stomach it when she got desperate for money and let herself believe Vincent's lies.

"I'm sorry, hon, I really am. Please don't be mad at me. The car insurance is due, and I lost two houses this month. He pays well, and, most of the time, he's not so bad." She fingered the yellow-green puffiness under her shining black gaze. "I hate that I've disappointed you again."

"Don't cry!" Panicked, he rushed forward and put his arm around her slender shoulders, already standing a head taller than her and not even fourteen yet. Someday, he vowed, he would be big enough and old enough to give that man a taste of his own medicine. "Sit down and I'll finish dinner." He tried easing her onto the worn sofa in front of the television that hadn't worked in over a month, but she didn't budge. "What?"

She shook her head, sending her waist-length braid swinging. "He'll be here any minute. His wife…"

"Shit, I don't want to hear it."

"Don't swear."

"Don't screw him," he shot back then swore under his breath when she blanched. "Sorry," he mumbled, shamefaced.

That rich married asshole was the only person who could push him to the point of showing such disrespect to his mother. Wiyaka was full-blooded Indian, half Sioux, half Hopi, and even though they'd left the reservation several years ago, she had continued to raise him in the ways of their people, including to respect his elders.

"You're such a good boy, Dakota. I don't deserve you. If only I could give you the life you deserve." Her youthful face reflected the aching sadness he often heard in her voice.

"All I need is you." He never asked who the white man was who had fathered him, never cared enough to know. She'd mentioned a few men who "helped" her get jobs and a place to live when she'd set out on her own but had never offered more than that. Heavy footsteps clomping down the hall of their run-down apartment building propelled him toward the door. "I'll return when he's gone."

Dakota didn't look back as he stormed out and took the emergency exit to the stairs that led down to the rear alley, but some sixth sense urged him not to go far. They lived in a poor part of Phoenix, but it wasn't the gangs or riffraff that scared him. That slimy bastard who thought his money allowed him special privileges, like using a desperate young mother for rough sex and as a punching bag, worried the hell out of him.

He walked down to the street, paused then slid down the wall to sit and watch for Vincent to leave his building, and his mother. Night had fallen but not the temperature, and he was sweating in the arid heat, or maybe because he couldn't rid himself of the itch between his shoulders telling him all was not right.

An hour later, he stood just as Vincent dashed by without noticing him and jumped into his fancy car parked down the block. Alarmed at the older man's ashen face, Dakota ran inside and took the stairs two at a time. When he barged into their apartment, the metallic smell of blood almost sent him to his knees.

Panic and fear unlike anything he'd ever

experienced wrenched a cry from his stricken throat. "Mom!" Moving much slower, he went down the short hall and opened her bedroom door, his blood turning to ice in his veins at the red splatter that met his eyes before he saw his mother sprawled in a pool of blood on the bed. So much blood...

Dakota jerked awake with a gasp, running a shaky hand over his damp brow as he tried to calm his racing heart, the oath he'd made that night playing in his head. *Nothing and no one will stop me from seeking to avenge my mother's death.* "Fuck." Swinging his legs out from the twisted sheets, he got out of bed and grabbed his jeans from the foot, remembering that vow as clearly as if he'd made it yesterday. He yanked them on without bothering to get a pair of underwear and stormed out of the house. Pausing on the porch, he struggled to take a deep breath of cool midnight air but failed to get past the tight constriction of his throat to fill his lungs. Knowing there was only one thing that could help him shake the dregs of the nightmare of his mother's murder, he strode toward the horse stable.

He lifted a hand to Scotty, the cowhand on night duty, riding the perimeter of the barns, to let him know everything was fine. Any of the employees on the ranch he co-owned with his closest friends,

Shawn and Clayton, who had been with them longer than a few months, had seen him hit the stables wearing nothing but jeans in the dead of night.

Entering the ten-stalled barn, his body taut with rage, muscles quivering from holding himself in check, he strode straight to Phantom's stall. "Yeah, you're as ready as I am, aren't you, boy?" Grabbing a handful of the dark-dapple-gray Morgan's black mane, he swung up on his back and rode him outside. As soon as they cleared the stable yard, he nudged the stallion with his knees and bent low over his neck, relishing the fast takeoff and massive, bunching muscles under him.

Visions of his mother's blood-soaked body stretched out on her bed swam in his head as the ground sped by under Phantom's pounding hooves. The full moon offered enough illumination to make out the silhouette of far-off mountains and wooded areas to his right and left as they tore across the vast range. His straight, shoulder-length hair whipped around his face as he forced himself to pull up the image of Vincent's face as he'd last seen the man who had stabbed his mother to death. It was easy to do, as he would never forget and never rest until he'd exacted revenge. Not knowing anything else about him had made that quest difficult the last twenty-plus years, but that didn't deter him.

His impatience for justice had simmered the first decade when he'd been too young to do much, and the technology now available hadn't existed. The cops were no help, shoving his mother's case into the cold-case files just three months later.

The good priest, Father Joe, had stepped in to help him, Shawn, and Clayton when they had fled their abusive foster parent one night, contacting his friend, Buck Cooper to take them in. Relocating to Mountain Bend, Idaho from Phoenix, the only home he'd known, had been the best thing to happen to Dakota in a long time, but, back then, his rage had kept him from appreciating Father Joe's and Buck's inquiries on his behalf as much as he should have. He remembered hiding out in the woods when they skipped school, and Buck's "positive reinforcement" techniques of extra chores that worked better than any corporal discipline their former guardians had implemented.

Dakota tugged on Phantom's mane to slow the horse to a trot, his perspiration-damp body finally cooling, along with his rioting emotions from the rush of night air and rigorous gallop under the star-studded sky. His chest tightened as he recalled losing Buck to a massive heart attack a few years ago. He still missed the man he'd grown to love who had taught him so much, not only the ranching and farming business but how to deal with his anger issues without lashing out at those around him.

Yeah, he thought, turning Phantom around by pressing his knees into the Morgan's heaving sides, he owed Buck a lot. But not enough to discontinue his quest of unearthing Vincent's full name and whereabouts and making him pay for snuffing out his mother's young life.

Dakota had a life here in Idaho he loved, friends he cared a great deal for, who kept warning him about everything he would lose if he continued down his current path toward vengeance. Even knowing that included them, since both Shawn and Clayton were in law enforcement, he'd made a vow twenty-one years, eight months, and six days ago he still intended to honor.

Nothing and no one would stop him from seeking to avenge his mother's death.

*****

Poppy slipped out onto the front porch of her small cabin, still acclimating to her new, temporary home and the different climate. After arriving in

Idaho a few days ago, she didn't hesitate to jump right into her job overseeing the Bar S sheep ranch, enlisting the part-time college help when she had questions instead of going to her boss. The gruff man who had handed her the keys to the cabin, stating he'd show her around later, didn't realize who he had hired. Poppy wasn't one to sit idly by when she could get down to work, and she enjoyed taking the hands-on approach in learning the ropes of Jerry Sanders' operation as much as getting dirty tending his five-hundred-plus sheep herd. She'd seen little of her recalcitrant boss since then but had already informed him she wouldn't let him take his surly disposition out on her from here on out. He'd seemed surprised she called him on it but nodded in agreement. Life was too damn short to waste walking around on eggshells when there were things to do.

Settling in the rickety rocker she'd found exploring the barn loft, she gazed up at the inky sky and bright stars. Resting her head against the chair, she toed the porch and let the slow glide lull her into relaxing until movement beyond the wide expanse separating the cabin from the neighbor's pastureland caught her attention.

The silhouette forms of a horse and rider speeding across the field drew her to her feet as goose bumps popped up along her bare arms and legs. Intrigued, she jogged toward the fence line in bad need of repair and leaned on a post, squinting to get a better look in the shadows cast by the bright, full moon. Her breath caught as she made out the wild, pagan appearance of the bareback rider, a man as big as the horse carrying him over the rough ground at breakneck speed. How he managed to stay on, let alone control the animal was beyond her, but her heart flipped watching the sheer beauty of the pair with their manes flying about them.

They slowed then turned and headed back in the direction they'd come from at a much more sedate pace, the man's posture ramrod straight as he seemed to know his way around in the dark without pause.

Interesting neighbor, and one Poppy found herself fascinated by as she returned to the cabin with her pulse still pumping hotly.

CHAPTER ONE

Poppy rolled out of bed and glanced at the clock with a groan. A week later, and she was still waking from restless dreams about the neighboring midnight cowboy. Telling herself she was just horny after the past year of celibacy due to her illness wasn't working. Now she had to rush to meet with Jerry, who had finally decided he should go over a few things with her.

She got rid of the cobwebs standing under the hot shower, and, by the time she poured a cup of coffee and stepped outside into the bright glare of the morning sun, she was ready to take on the lion in his den. Other than he was a widower, she knew little about her boss, except the sixty-something-year-old man preferred solitude. According to comments from the part-time college hands she supervised, woe to anyone who bothered Sanders when he was in one of his snits.

Jerry's attitude didn't bother her. Everyone was entitled to bad days. What did bug her was the state of disrepair his barns and fencing were in, most of it from a lack of regular upkeep. Factor in age and weather, and the place was literally falling down around him. As she followed the path alongside a row of fragrant apple trees up to the back side of his house, she wondered why he didn't show more interest in his property. At least the livestock appeared to have ample food and water and basic care.

Instead of going around to the front and entering his office from the drive, she rapped on the back glass door then opened it a crack to call inside. "Morning, Jerry." She paused, waiting for him to appear, not surprised when she saw him round a corner and stomp through the living area toward the slider with a scowl. Smiling, she waved.

He slid the door wider, his gray hair in tufts, wire-framed glasses perched on his nose, and irritation evident in his snapping brown eyes. "You're late and at the wrong entrance. Go—"

"Nope. I need you to come out so I can show you everything that needs to get done." Poppy looked past him and spotted a large portrait of a beautiful woman hanging above the fireplace. "Is that your wife? I'm sorry for your loss." He'd never mentioned his marriage, but the pain flashing across his face before he masked it hinted at a possible reason for his surly disposition.

"Your job is to overlook the care of the sheep, not my property."

"I can't do a good job of that unless the animals have decent shelter that's not falling down around them, or fencing adequate enough to keep them safe from wild predators. Since I've been here, six have gone missing overnight, and we haven't found them. I'm assuming they were a wolf or wildcat's dinner." She sipped her coffee and let that sink in. His wince indicated he cared, which gave her hope he would come out of his funk enough to start repairs.

Jerry huffed. "Fine. Let's go." He came out the door, a black-and-white border collie dashing out behind him. "Great. Now Otis will want to tag along, and I'll never get him back inside."

"Why didn't you tell me you have a working dog?" She stretched a hand out to Otis, who licked her fingers, his tail whipping back and forth before he took off toward the barns. "It looks like he's eager to work."

"He stays with me."

Poppy opened her mouth to argue then clamped it shut again, seeing the way he watched the dog with longing. She suspected Otis was the only companion he had allowed himself since losing his wife, and he now couldn't bear to separate from the dog. She never imagined she would need to fall back on her psychology education as well as her animal husbandry when she accepted this job.

"Okay, but if you don't agree to get someone out here to fix the fences and replace the roof on the shelter ASAP, I'm going to borrow him to round up your sheep when they take off." She left that threat out there as they reached the barn and sheep housing, and she saw how happy Otis was out in the pasture, running circles around the flock, and the good job he did keeping the babies close to their ewes.

By the time Jerry returned to the house, taking Otis with him, he'd reluctantly agreed to get someone out to work on repairs. Poppy decided she had to be content with that for now, and turned her attention to brushing up on shearing, which would start soon.

*****

Poppy braced her arms on the fence rail and laughed when Nathan, one of the hands, released the young sheep and the now wool-free ewe bolted, as if a pack of coyotes were on her tail. As cute as she thought the sheep were with full, curly coats, they were even more adorable shaved. She was glad she had arrived at the Bar S in time to witness the spring wool-gathering, a daunting, time-consuming process, she mused as another one was let go to dart into the pasture. She was equally happy her duties didn't include helping with the physically demanding chore. As good as she was feeling, there was no way she possessed the strength and stamina needed to wrestle a three-hundred-pound male Merino sheep or even one half that size.

Stifling a sigh of self-pity, she pushed away from the fence. With a thumbs-up gesture of approval to Mick, an older man Jerry hired to oversee both the process and gathering of wool, she left the corral and returned to her cabin where she slid behind the wheel of her cherry-red Outlander Sport. One of the perks of her corporate management job had been the high-end pay that made purchasing the SUV possible. As much as she enjoyed all the bells and whistles that had come with the manager of acquisitions position she'd held, and their support in keeping her on and then giving her a year to decide if she wanted to return, she didn't miss her last job in Houston. Changing careers to ranch manager and making the move to Idaho to work in the complete opposite capacity of what she'd been doing for almost three years had boosted her spirits in the two weeks she'd been here. Whether from the outdoor, fresh-air work environment, spending more time with animals than people, or the change of scenery from heavy traffic and congested buildings to wide-open spaces and small towns, she didn't know and didn't waste time analyzing the data.

Life was too short to piddle away hours on meaningless endeavors, especially when there was still so much to learn, to do, to enjoy.

Like figure out who their sexy neighbor was, and why she couldn't forget seeing him that night. The dark silhouette of untamed wildness the pair had portrayed matched her restless spirit and left her itching to solve the mystery of his identity. She could ask Jerry, but it was more fun to prolong her interest and curiosity. Dragging out her quest to learn more about him would help occupy her mind and divert her from the constant fidgetiness she lived with. It was a curse to grow restless and bored easily, to need stimulating, new experiences to stay satisfied.

Poppy drove toward the small town of Mountain Bend, recalling the day she'd received the cancer diagnosis and how she'd tried to dispel the grip of fear cramping her abdomen while attempting to lighten the grave expressions on her parents' faces. *Come on, Mom, Dad, you know I've been craving a new challenge lately.* She winced, remembering that flippant remark, and the tears swimming in her mother's eyes because she always suspected Poppy's glib shallowness hid her insecurities. Poppy never wasted time trying to analyze why she couldn't stick with one thing for long or one person. She was happy with who she was and didn't want to change.

Which was why she'd never let on how difficult the chemo treatments and the rejected bone marrow transplants were for her to cope with. Until now, she'd been blessed with near-perfect health that afforded her a physically active lifestyle rife with mentally stimulating challenges. The disappointment and worry those rejections caused her, and the weeks of lying around too sick to do anything except flick through channels on the television or sleep, had taken an emotional toll she'd struggled to hide from the two people she loved the most.

Put it to rest, Flynn. That was Poppy's standard rebuke whenever she found herself edging toward self-pity. Switching gears, she slowed, yielding to a small group of white-tailed deer sprinting across the road. She loved watching their sleek, graceful forms and envied their freedom and ability to spend their days running across the prairies. Outside of Houston, it was easy to find this kind of space and wildlife, but her busy schedule hadn't allowed much time to take those long, leisurely drives. Here, she could relax and enjoy a sunny afternoon in the country while still working. The shearing gave her an opportunity to fill Jerry's list from the feedstore and pick up a hamburger with the works. She never missed an opportunity to indulge the return of her appetite.

Passing the city limits sign for Mountain Bend, Poppy couldn't help grinning reading population 2603, the same reaction as when she'd entered the small town the first time upon arriving. Once she returned home, she would make a point of taking day trips to scout out the rural towns in Southeast Texas. Maybe she would find one she liked enough to move there, close enough to visit her parents regularly, big enough to find a job. With her experience now including ranching, she shouldn't have too much trouble.

Providing she stayed healthy.

Following Jerry's directions, Poppy drove down Main Street and made a note to run into the mom-and-pop grocery on her way out after visiting a few of the quaint gift shops and the library. Turning at the end of Main, she found the drive-through burger joint she remembered seeing and idled at the large, mouth-watering menu.

"Order when ready," a young girl's voice piped through the speaker.

Feeling adventurous, Poppy chose something new to test her reawakened taste buds. "I'll have a half-pound buffalo burger with cheese, fries, and iced tea, please."

Following the girl's instructions, she pulled forward and grabbed her purse off the passenger seat. As soon as the girl slid back the partition, Poppy salivated from the aromas wafting in her window. "I hope my order is as good as that smells. I've never eaten buffalo meat," she said, handing over payment.

"You'll love it. Pete puts his special seasoning in them, and the cheese is made locally, the fries from fresh potatoes, not frozen."

Poppy flashed her a grin. "He ought to hire you to make an ad."

"He's my dad, and he's paying for college, which is compensation enough, not to mention he's a darn good cook. Here you go. I hope you come back."

Taking the bag and paper cup, she replied, "Thanks, I'm sure I will."

With her stomach rumbling, she drove the half block to the feedstore and parked out front before delving into the bag. "Oh, man, just as good as it smells." She moaned, chewing her first bite. The sandwich was huge, so she ate half then went for the fries, closing her eyes in ecstasy as she tasted the difference between fresh and frozen. "Okay, these I'm going to pig out on and to heck with saving some for later."

When she got down to four fat fries, she took a long drink of tea and slid out of her vehicle, carrying the carton with her as she strode toward the front door with her head down. Intent on shoving two more in her mouth, she didn't notice someone exiting the store until she plowed into a towering brick wall.

"*Oooomph!*" With her mouth full, she looked up, way up, as a pair of large, calloused hands wrapped around her upper arms, and said the first thing that popped into her head. "Oh my. I would apologize but I'm not really sorry."

The man's black Stetson shielded his eyes but not his sun-darkened, swarthy complexion, taut jaw, and enticing lips frowning with irritation. At five foot eight, she wasn't used to craning her neck to get a good look at a man. His displeasure didn't deter her hormones from going haywire at the breadth of his wide shoulders stretching a black T-shirt, the bulge of his biceps as he held her, and the very brief brush of her chest against his rock-hard pecs.

"You should watch where you're going instead of stuffing your face."

He should be on the cover of one of those smutty romance novels. And that's where her imagination took her—straight into the smut department. The deep rumble of his voice went right to her pussy, and she grinned, loving this little pick-me-up to her day. "How about if I make the supreme sacrifice and give you my last two?" She shook the fries.

"Unbelievable," he muttered, releasing her arms and stepping back. "Ma'am." With a mocking tip of his hat brim, he spun on his booted heels and stomped over to a truck big enough to hold his large frame.

"Whew!" Poppy fanned herself as she eyed his tight backside in snug denim and decided the man looked as good walking away as he did standing in front of her.

She shrugged when he got behind the wheel and pulled away without looking back once then put him out of her mind and ate the last two fries herself. Going inside, she wound through the aisles of feed and nutrients for ranch and farm animals until she found the sales counter and handed the middle-aged, balding man Jerry's order.

"Hi. I'm Poppy from the Sanders ranch. Jerry sent me to get this order filled and have you deliver it, tomorrow, if possible. And also to get the name of a good contractor for repairs." That last was a lie. Jerry's procrastinating to make good on his agreement to see to the neglected housing forced her to take matters into her own hands.

"Heard tell Old Man Sanders finally hired another manager. I think I wagered twenty you wouldn't last a month. Name's Bill." He took the list with a friendly nod.

"People are betting on how long before I quit or before I'm fired?" she returned dryly, amused by his disclosure.

"Quit. No one lasts until the cantankerous fool fires 'em." A shadow darkened Bill's blue eyes. "I guess most folks around here don't blame him, though, not after the missus died in that accident. At least he's finally showing an interest in his property again. That's a positive sign."

"That is rough. Was it recently, then?"

"Goin' on three years now, if I remember right," he answered, tallying up the order. "Nice woman. I've got all this in stock, so tell him he'll have it tomorrow afternoon." He handed her the charge receipt, along with a large Saran Wrapped bone. "For Otis. And here's Lloyd's card. Jerry must have misplaced his number. He used to use Lloyd for upkeep work all the time."

"He didn't say." Which was true. "Otis will love the bone. Thanks." She had only managed to get the dog away from her boss twice in the last ten days. Another thing she needed to convince Jerry to do. Otis loved his job herding the sheep and deserved the treat for his hard work.

"Nice to meet you, miss."

"I hope you still feel the same when you lose that bet. After three-and-a-half weeks, I don't see me leaving any time soon."

Bill chuckled. "You might be good for Jerry."

"We'll see."

Poppy loved a challenge, and sticking with her ill-tempered boss for a while might require the grit and stamina she hadn't bothered applying to her previous jobs once she'd grown restless. It would be fun to learn who else around town was in on the bet then decide who she liked best and make sure he or she won.

Returning to Main Street, she parked in front of the library, her pulse leaping as she caught sight of the tall hunk she'd run into earlier now coming out of the sheriff's office with a deputy. *Wow*. The double whammy of tall, dark, and panty-creaming sexy conjured up all kinds of naughty thoughts. She squirmed in her seat, her body heating as her silk panties slid against the sensitive exposure of her bare pubis. The months of chemo treatments had not only turned her head bald but stripped all of her body hair away. The one and only perk to the debilitating drugs was discovering nerve endings hidden since puberty, very responsive nerves to the slightest touch. She'd gotten such an uplifting kick out of that, she now kept herself shaved.

It was easier to get a better look at the large cowboy from this short distance and notice his American Indian heritage in his copper tone and straight black hair pulled back in a leather tie at his nape. Another man came out of the office next to the sheriff's, settling a dark-brown Stetson on his sandy hair as he joined the other two. Good grief, she could sit here and ogle sexy-as-sin cowboys all day and not get bored if they all resembled those three.

With a nod, the tallest one she'd dubbed as hers went to his truck as his friends got into a sheriff's cruiser. It was just her luck when her guy glanced over the top of his truck and nailed her in place with a direct gaze. Unable to help herself again, she grinned, lifting a hand in a finger wave, somehow sensing he would see right through any attempt to pretend she'd just noticed him. Instead of returning her gesture, he shook his head and opened the door. Her stare was as astute as his, and she glimpsed the one-sided tilt of his mouth as he got behind the wheel. Satisfied with that, she hopped out of her vehicle and strode into the library without looking his way again.

****

Dakota eyed the redhead's twitching ass as she entered the library, wondering who the hell she was. Having lived in the area for twenty years, he recognized almost everyone, with the exception of tourists. He doubted anyone passing through would need to shop at the feed store, but, given her cheeky attitude, he wouldn't discount that oddity. Her brazenness annoyed him as he preferred demure women content to do his bidding at the club. Somehow, he couldn't picture her in the only role he engaged with women, submissive to his sexual dominance.

It was a good thing she wasn't even close to his type, he decided, pulling away from the curb to follow

Shawn and Clayton to the restaurant for lunch. For starters, the fiery-red curls framing her thin face were way too short to get a good grip on, a useful tool for exerting control. The dark circles under her bright-blue eyes diminished that attractive feature, the devil-may-care, somewhat taunting attitude she portrayed rubbed him wrong, and she was too skinny for his taste.

Not that he was interested, he told himself. Parking in front of the area's most popular dining establishment, a renovated mining facility, he shut down thoughts of the new face in town and joined his two closest friends at the door. "I take it Sharon is working," he said to Clayton, who held the door open. Normally, they preferred the local bar, the Watering Hole, when they got together for lunch, but whenever the twice-divorced waitress whom Clayton couldn't shake after a few dates was scheduled to work, he refused to go there.

"You got it. Why aren't you meeting Lisa for lunch?" Clayton asked Shawn.

"Faculty luncheon." The sun reflected off Shawn's deputy badge clipped to his waist as he followed Dakota inside, asking him, "Did you notice how he deftly changed the subject?"

"Obvious as all get out." Dakota spotted an

empty table and led the way past the buffet line.

Ignoring their poke at him, Clayton stuck with his change of topic. "How is she coping, learning her own brother was the one terrorizing her?"

His blue eyes shone with concern as they took their seats, but Dakota noticed Clayton continued to keep quiet about the mistake he'd made in dating Sharon after he and Shawn had warned him.

Shawn sent Dakota a knowing grin before answering. "I'm helping her work through it. We're planning a trip to Phoenix as soon as school lets out. Father Joe wants to see for himself she's all right."

His training in law enforcement had come in handy last week when Shawn had saved the new teacher he'd been seeing from a stalker, sustaining a flesh wound he'd already recovered from in the process. Dakota had been more than happy to be in on the takedown of that greedy bastard, even though he'd seen how Bruce Pomeroy's death weighed on Lisa's mind.

"I can't get away, but we should pitch in and send Father a plane ticket to come here for a visit. It's been ages since he made the trip," Clayton suggested.

"I can't make the trip now, either. Did you remember I'm picking up my new mare this weekend?" He was looking forward to breeding Morgan horses, using Phantom's rare, larger size to start the process.

Shawn waited until they placed their order to question Dakota's decision to tackle yet another job when he had his hands full with running the ranch already. "Are you sure you want to take on more work? With my campaign and Clayton's court schedule, our time is limited for lending a hand, even more so than ever."

"Are you sure you want to run for sheriff?" Dakota shot back, knowing Shawn was still on the fence about jumping into politics and aiming for the higher position, the extra paperwork and political ass-kissing that usually came with the job, two big deterrents he'd admitted he was still wrestling with. "Like you, I won't know until I try. If it's too time consuming, I'm not out anything and will have a few new horses to add to our stables. Don't worry, I'll still put in hours Friday and Saturday night managing Spurs."

The three of them had purchased the private club from the owner, Randy Daniels, a few weeks ago. Dakota recalled Randy's hurt and anger over his wife's infidelity that led to their recent divorce, prompting him to sell the club he'd built, leaving him free to nurse his wounds away from all the memories of his marriage. *Poor schmuck.* The breakup and betrayal of their six-year union was just one more reason Dakota steered clear of women intent on a serious relationship.

"Are there any subs left you haven't run off?"

Dakota shrugged, used to Clayton's teasing remarks. "There are always those who think to reform the big, bad Indian, or the ones who find out soon enough they can't goad me into anything except walking away when they push for more than I think is wise."

"You could try turning them down nicely," Shawn drawled, taking the plate the waitress handed him upon her return.

"I'm not nice, remember?"

Their server smirked as she set his plate down. "I remember, if they don't," she said but walked away grinning.

Dakota jerked a thumb toward her. "She doesn't mind my attitude."

Clayton picked up a fry as he taunted, "What's her name?"

Scowling, he racked his brain. "Mandy, Mary, something like that."

"You're such a moron. Try Melissa," Shawn

filled in with a derisive look.

Ignoring both of them, Dakota bit into his club sandwich as he found himself wondering what the redhead's name was then uttered a curse for even thinking about her. He needed to get back to the ranch and work, confident his curiosity was a temporary annoyance.

Dakota returned to the ranch Buck had left to the three of them, eager to start the searches on two more Vincents he'd come across in his quest to avenge his mother's death. He hadn't mentioned them to Clayton and Shawn, since there was no point. His well-meaning friends would try again to talk him out of his quest, and he would refuse, so why bother discussing the new leads? The pricey-but-worth-it advanced search engine he'd installed on his computer did a lot of the work for him, but, so far, twenty-eight out of forty-six men he had dug up with the first name of Vincent living in Phoenix at that time were dead ends.

He would never forget the man's face and would never stop looking. A two-decade-old memory and first name weren't much to go on, even though the detective in charge of his mother's case, Trey Jansen, had him work with a sketch artist. Years ago, Dakota had taken that image and scanned it into the computer then ran it through his identity program to generate an updated image of what Vincent would look like now. He kept in touch with Detective Jansen, shunning the older man's cautions over becoming too zealous in his campaign for justice.

The man he remembered seeing come to their apartment then leaving at a frantic run covered in blood was still breathing, walking around free, and that was something he wouldn't accept. Not now or ever.

Pulling in front of the farmhouse he'd called home since the gruff, strict cowboy who owned the Rolling Hills Ranch had taken in three surly fifteen-year-old boys and shaped them into the men they were today, he took a moment to scan the activity around the stables and barns. Buck had taken stock of Dakota's attitude, the chip on his shoulder he'd refused to relinquish, and set about showing him how to channel his anger into hard work. Resentment didn't begin to cover what had gone through him those first weeks living under Buck's soft-spoken orders, but he wouldn't trade his education on the ranch and the Coopers' positive influence on his life for anything. Without the hard work, encouragement, and praise from Buck, and the motherly support of his wife, Betty, he would have continued down the same self-destructive path of venting his fury over his mother's brutal death by lashing out at everyone around him.

Getting out of his truck, he lifted a hand to two cowhands as they mounted and rode toward the herd grazing in the nearest pasture. The young men Buck had employed who now worked for Dakota were a close-knit group, keeping an eye on each other, and got on well together, much like he, Clayton, and Shawn. Something had clicked between them the first time they'd met under Doyle Atkins' roof. They had bonded quickly after learning they were each orphaned in recent months, were the same age, and resented the authority of strangers who knew nothing about them.

Jogging up the front steps to the wraparound porch, a rare grin tugged at his lips as he recalled the bets they'd taken on who would be the first to return one of Doyle's punches. Dakota had won, of course, his temper giving way to a solid gut punch the second time Doyle backhanded him. It was a good thing they'd already cemented their plan to sneak away from that foster home later that week, as he never doubted Doyle would have followed through on his threat to see him in juvenile hall.

The quiet of his house suited Dakota, and

he entered, wondering why anyone would prefer otherwise. Chaos annoyed him, as did a lot of inane chatter and unnecessary noise, which made it a good thing he planned to stay single. Shawn could have the committed relationship. Clayton would keep him company when he wanted it, as he enjoyed playing the field too much to give it up for one woman.

A too-thin face surrounded by fiery-red curls popped up again as he strode to his desk in the corner of the living room. "That's annoying," he muttered, pulling out the chair. He shoved the memory of the woman aside, sat down, and booted up his searches on the two new names he'd added. Images popped up, along with their last names, ages, and professions. As far as personal data, that's all he could get without enlisting Trey's help or getting into illegal hacking. He wouldn't lie, he mused, leaning back in the chair to scrutinize the photos for any resemblance to the man he remembered. The temptation to take that risk kept getting harder and harder to refuse, despite all he now had to lose.

Dakota bent forward to get a better look at the Vincent on the right. The eyes were the closest resemblance he'd come across yet. With a few clicks, he sent that image into another program then left the computer to work its magic, coming up with a possible image of the man twenty years ago. As he strode from the house toward the stables to saddle up, he wished the hands of justice didn't move so slow.

CHAPTER TWO

Storming up to Jerry's back door, Poppy didn't try to hide her frustration. It took only one sharp knock to bring him into the room. Without waiting for his invite, she entered his house, too angry with him to admire the tidy interior.

"I didn't say you could come inside."

"I didn't ask," she shot back. Softening her tone, she called to the dog. "Otis, come."

"Where are you taking my dog?"

She noticed he wasn't trying to stop her, let alone fire her. He grumbled a lot but didn't seem to mind sparring with her. Poppy figured no one, except maybe his late wife, had ever stood up to him, and he wasn't sure what to do about her.

"To round up *your* sheep that got out of *your* downed fences again. Have you called Lloyd yet?" She reached down to pet Otis, never taking her eyes off Jerry's face. "Damn it, Jerry. Why not?" she asked when he tightened his mouth.

"I haven't got time. I'll get to it. Ask the guys to mend the fence."

"They're too busy doing other chores during the

few hours you give them. It takes time to tend over five hundred sheep. You should remember that from the days you worked your flock yourself." Poppy locked her back teeth to contain her frustration, looking away from his stubborn expression. Daring a glance toward the portrait, she noticed the chess set sitting on a table below it, in front of the fireplace, a chair placed on each side.

"You need to go. Bring Otis back when you're done," he demanded, a note of desperation coloring his voice.

"You played chess with your wife. What was her name?" She refused to back down under his glare.

They engaged in a battle of wills, staring at each other until he sighed with an annoyed grumble. "You are something, girl. Her name was Amanda. Now, go away."

An idea formed, but before pissing him off further, she needed to ask about a mount. "Which horse can I handle easiest? Keep in mind, I haven't ridden in over a year." Another activity she had missed a lot in the past year due to her health. She'd been a regular at the nearest riding facility back home for several years and wondered if her favorite horse, Goldie, missed her.

"Take Hank. If you can ride, you can handle

him. *Now* go away," he insisted, crossing his arms in a defiant stance.

"Hank it is." She grinned and patted his shoulder. "Buck up, Jerry. This evening, I plan to beat the pants off you in chess." She dashed out before he could refuse, shutting the door behind her with a wide smile, quite pleased with herself.

Poppy hiked to the barn that provided stalls for the horses, in addition to storage for hay and feed, checking inside the fenced sheep pens that enclosed their shelters for ample feed and clean water. Most of the flock spent the day grazing the pastureland, but there were always those kept penned due to recent births or recovering from an injury.

Watching Otis run on ahead, she wished she possessed half the stamina the dog enjoyed, hoping this job with its physical demands was a start in that direction. Of the three horses Jerry owned, Hank stood the shortest, appeared less energetic when out in the pasture with the two mares, and had resisted every overture from her since she had arrived. He would have been her last pick, but Jerry knew his livestock better than her, and she would heed his advice.

After retrieving a saddle from the tack room, she carried it to the corral, whistling for Hank. The mares trotted over as she entered, but Hank just stood by the feed bin, chewing slowly while giving her an indifferent look. "So, this is how we're going to start, huh?" Determined to win the small Pinto over, she approached him, holding out the sugar cube she'd picked up in the barn. His gaze sharpened, his ears picking up as he lumbered toward her. She figured he was a typical male, and the way to his heart was through his stomach.

Hank remained docile, eating the treat as she clipped the reins to his halter and led him to the rail where she'd left the saddle. He behaved while she saddled him, swung onto his back, and leaned over to open the gate. She relaxed as he walked with a nice, slow gait at her booted nudge, and she turned him to follow the fence line until they reached the downed section. With another whistle, Otis came running and led the way onto the neighboring property where she'd spotted their white sheep mingling with a herd of black Angus cattle early this morning.

Poppy enjoyed riding a horse again, the sun warming her shoulders and the fresh air ripe with the scent of spring, but not as much as she liked the view of a tall cowboy wearing black from his Stetson down to his boots, astride a large stallion as dark as he. She paused a moment on her way across the pasture to watch his expertise in handling the big charcoal-gray horse, and it suddenly dawned on her she was looking at her midnight rider.

As she prompted Hank into moving again, she thought there was something else familiar about him. It wasn't until she rode close enough to make out his rugged face she put two and two together. Sudden recognition of him as the same man she'd run into at the feedstore jolted her with a wave of pleasant sexual awareness, and her brain instantly dragged him into her gutter of smutty fantasies.

Either her unexpected yank on the reins or something else caused Hank to switch abruptly from a docile mount to an agitated, irritated horse. Before Poppy could switch gears and get her mind back on task, he bucked his hind end, her inattention and unpreparedness causing her to lose her balance on a horse for the first time in years.

With a startled cry, Poppy toppled to the ground, getting the wind knocked out of her as she landed on her back. The approach of pounding horse hooves shook the earth under her then a pair of broad shoulders and a glowering, drop-dead gorgeous face blocked the blue sky above her. Even while struggling to get her breath back, she couldn't help smiling in giddy pleasure.

Hard hands helped her up as he rumbled in a deep voice, "Your sheep are trespassing."

Since she caught a hint of concern in that annoyed statement, she dismissed his complaint with an equally inane comment. "Your cattle are mingling with my sheep."

He seemed to get a good look at her as she stood, one hand keeping hold of her arm while he swept the other across her ribs and around to her back. "You," he growled, his acknowledgement of their prior meeting sounding like an accusation.

"Yep, me. *Oh.*" Her breath caught as he brushed off her butt then she leaned forward, widening her grin. "I think you missed a spot." His huff of exasperation amused her, and she patted his rock-hard chest. "Lighten up. Life's too short to go around wound up so tightly."

"I wouldn't be wound up so tightly if you didn't keep showing up like a thorn in my side," he bit out. "If you're not hurt, I'll help you gather your livestock. I'm Dakota Smith, in case Old Man Sanders hasn't told you. And you are?"

"Poppy Flynn," she answered, stepping back and reaching for Hank's reins when he released her arm. "And, no, Jerry hasn't mentioned you."

"What the hell kind of name is Poppy?" he

asked in derision.

Okay, that disparagement irked Poppy. His continued discourtesy chipped away at her good humor, and she snapped, "What the hell kind of name is Dakota?"

He thumbed the brim of his hat up enough for her to get a good look into his coal-black eyes. "An honored family name, passed down through generations."

So, she touched a raw nerve. At this point, she didn't care. "Well, I'm a colorful flower."

"You're colorful, I'll give you that. Come on, let's get to work."

He sighed, and her annoyance dropped away. "If we leave them long enough, we could start a livestock breed of doodles."

"Don't even think it."

Poppy gave up trying to get a smile out of Dakota. Instead, she mounted Hank, making sure she kept a good grip on the reins, and rode toward the herd without another word or looking at him again.

****

Dakota followed Poppy, eyeing her decent seat

on Sanders' pinto, and wondered why her perky personality rubbed him wrong. He swore he wasn't petty enough to feel that way because it was irritating to find himself interested in what caused the bruised shadows under her blue eyes. He realized redheads were often pale, but her complexion showed a pallor that went beyond natural skin tone, or so it appeared to him. She was too skinny and too brash for his taste, yet he liked her quirky sense of humor.

Go figure.

He watched his two ranch hands, Rick and Casey, grin as she attempted to cut the sheep from the herd, and it became obvious the dog knew more than she. When they started toward her, he raised a hand to stop them, nudging Phantom her way. She was his problem, not theirs.

"Hank isn't wired for this," he told her as he pulled up alongside the pinto. "Let me and the dog separate them for you."

"I want to learn. Can you give me some pointers?"

Stubborn, but he couldn't fault her for wanting to acquire more skill. "You don't have the right mount. Doesn't Sanders have a couple of mustangs?"

Ever since Sanders' wife died, his neighbor had become a recluse, venturing into town only when he needed something. Whenever they did meet up, he seemed to go out of his way to be difficult and rude. At first, everyone was understanding, given his loss, but, after a while, most people, including him, just stayed clear of the man. He'd been surprised when Poppy referred to him as Jerry. Sanders had insisted on no familiarity, and that included simple things, such as using his first name.

"Yes, but Jerry told me to ride Hank when I mentioned I haven't ridden for over a year. I'm good with him for now." She leaned forward to pat Hank's neck.

Dakota couldn't help but admire her determination not to give up, even if it would prolong getting the job done. "Okay, I can show you a few things as long as it doesn't take too much time. You'll find it harder because that horse isn't going to help, and I have my own work to finish."

Poppy shook her head, sending him a derisive glance. "Can't just offer to do something nice, can you? I'm a fast learner, so let's get to it. I have other work, also."

That remark shouldn't have caused guilt to tighten his gut, and because it did, his annoyance stayed in place as he showed her how to maneuver the horse and work with the dog. His cattle dog had died several months ago, still herding at age fifteen. He missed Cutter, an Australian Shepherd, and hadn't gotten around to replacing him yet. Watching Sanders' dog labor with such efficiency, though, made him think it was time he looked into getting another one.

"That was good," he called over as she successfully cut two sheep out of the cattle to join the three others, even though her mount was no help.

Her face brightened with a proud grin. "Told you I was a fast learner."

She was, but he could also see the strain the mental and physical challenge put her under reflected on her face. He wondered why she had applied for such a taxing job if she wasn't used to rigorous activity then decided that was Old Man Sanders' problem.

Turning Phantom to the right, away from Poppy, he looked over his shoulder. "I'll get the last two. Make sure that fence gets repaired so we don't have to do this again." Her eyes sparked, which gave him an odd sense of satisfaction. Facing forward, he rode toward the two ewes grazing docilely smack dab in the middle of animals three times their size. "Senseless critters," he muttered, as annoyed with the extra task as he was with his unaccustomed interest and concern for Poppy.

There was no time in his busy schedule for anything but a short break from work to indulge his sexual preference for dominance, which was what made purchasing the club worth the money and extra time. Going through a mental list of favorite subs, Dakota thought of a few he was confident would take his mind off the neighbor this weekend.

"Hey, Boss. Was that Sanders' new manager?" Rick asked as he and Casey joined him.

"So she says. Let's get this herd moving to the south pasture before we have any more delays."

Casey wiggled his eyebrows with a teasing leer. "I love a woman with long legs."

"Concentrate on work now, women later," Dakota insisted. The last thing he needed was his hired hands falling all over themselves to get Poppy's attention.

At thirty-five, he wasn't too old to remember how he had thought more with his dick than his brain during his early twenties, like Rick and Casey. As long as they put in a decent day's work, he didn't care how they spent their off time, and normally didn't mind the colorful talk and jokes the guys bandied about during the day. For some unfathomable reason, Casey's innocent remark had rankled, which added to the annoyance of his interrupted day.

"Hard to think straight knowing there's eye candy like that next door." Rick let out a dramatic sigh before heeding Dakota's glower and sending him a sharp salute with a tip of his hat. "On it, Boss."

Dakota berated himself for acting a hard ass then spent the next two hours driving the herd of a couple hundred head to a range with greener grass and a large pond. His mood didn't improve, even though he was outdoors, doing the work he loved. He couldn't seem to keep from wondering if Poppy managed to get the ewes back where they belonged without further issues, or why he even cared, which irked him. He had enough on his mind as it was, and there was no need to act neighborly by checking up on her. After all, it was her job to manage Sanders' flock.

"Maybe Rick and I should check on the neighbor, Boss. You know, make sure she returned the sheep without any problems," Casey suggested halfway back to the barns, his eyes lit with an eagerness that spoke of wanting more than to ensure the sheep wouldn't wander again any time soon.

Dakota stifled a grumble of impatience, thinking that was his responsibility even though Casey had given him the perfect opening to delegate the chore to them. If either wanted to pursue the damn woman on his own time, that was fine by him but not when there was still work to finish before the sun went down.

"You two go on in and finish at the stables with the others while I check on Sanders' employee," he instructed, hoping to avoid any more time-consuming delays interrupting his days by seeing that the sheep were where they belonged now, and his ranch hands stayed focused on their jobs while at work.

"Aw, shucks, Boss. Let us have some fun," Rick whined.

"I thought you were seeing someone, Rick."

"I am," he said with an unconcerned shrug that maddened Dakota. "But I'm not hog-tied to her. A guy's gotta keep his options open."

"Just don't string her along, or lie," he lectured, thinking of his mother and how long she'd believed Vincent's lies. "As for now, you can have all the fun you like on your own time. I'll catch up with you shortly."

He'd broken several hearts at that age while sowing his wild oats, but he'd always been upfront about his noncommitment intentions. His interest might not lean toward forming a relationship with a woman, or even bothering with getting to know someone beyond their sexual needs for a short time, but the love and respect Buck and Miss Betty had exhibited had shown Dakota what his mother had missed out on. His size, insistence on total sexual control, and brutal honesty in warning a woman against expecting anything else from him other than a scene or two at Spurs often sent them scampering away before anything got started. That never bothered him, as there was always another willing to accept his terms.

Life had been rough living on the reservation as a fatherless half-breed, and he'd gotten into more than his fair share of scrapes by the time he was ten and his mother moved them into Phoenix. Dakota had been much happier until Vincent had come along. He would take the soul-crushing guilt of knowing he was the reason Wiyaka left the safety of the reservation only to end up murdered to his grave. Finding the man who had treated her with such callous disregard then stolen her from him and making him pay would only avenge his mother's death. He doubted anything would alleviate the pain of his gut-wrenching loss.

Steering Phantom toward the Sanders' property, he rode through the woods dividing their land and came out at the fence line. The last thing he needed was more guilt to contend with, and that was why he was intent on making sure Poppy got back without mishap, given the strain on her features, no other reason.

As soon as he caught sight of her, he cursed. "What the hell is she doing now?" he muttered, seeing Poppy's bright-red head bent over a rail she was struggling to hold while using a nail gun to fasten it to the post. Remembering how drawn she'd appeared hours earlier, he couldn't believe she was still hard at work. From the looks of the newer boards already up, she hadn't taken a break between returning the sheep and getting started on mending the downed fencing, which shouldn't fall on her shoulders.

She glanced around as he rode up, her face flushed, her blue eyes widening in surprise before going to narrowed slits as she took in his displeasure.

"If you're not going to be nice, go away," she demanded as he dismounted.

"I am going to be nice by finishing this for you while you go sit down over there." He pointed to a grassy area in the shade, noting her damp face and pinched mouth.

Straightening, she glared at him as if affronted

by his offer. "I didn't ask for your help, nor do I need it."

"You look like shit, so you didn't need to ask." She winced at his blunt remark, but hurt feelings were better than watching her keel over with exhaustion. "Why did you take a job you're not physically able to handle in the first place?" he asked, plucking the nail gun from her hand. "And, since when is mending fences a sheep manager's job?"

"Since I didn't trust my boss to get it done before they escaped again and annoyed the neighbor."

She reached for the nail gun, but he dropped it and grabbed her around the waist, lifting her onto the rail that was secure. "Stay put or you may not like how I retaliate." Instead of responding to that threat with feminine outrage, like he'd expected, a slow smile curled her soft lips, her eyes sparking with an interested gleam that went straight to his cock.

Poppy leaned forward and cooed, "*Oooh*, now you've made me curious. What do you do with naughty girls, Mr. Smith?"

An image of her bright-red head dangling over his legs as she lay face down across his lap jumped into Dakota's head. His cock stirred again, but he tamped down his base instinct to deflect her antics by giving her a taste of what she was asking for. Instead, he opted for what always worked when he wanted to rid himself of a pesky attachment – intimidation.

Stepping up to the fence brought him eye level with her face and close enough for their body heat to warm them. He braced his hands on the fence post at her hips, and almost smiled when her throat worked as she swallowed with a look of wariness.

"It's not good to poke at a bear with a sore paw, baby. You never know when one will turn on you. Now, stay put and"—he reached for the pouch of nails at her side—"hand me these when I need them. I'll finish this section then have a word with Old Man Sanders myself about his property obligations."

Dakota wasn't sure what was going on in that head of hers as he watched her eyes turn stormy and her jaw tighten before she relaxed with a smile that didn't appear at all subdued, as he'd wanted.

With a sharp, two-fingered salute off her brow, Poppy drawled, "Aye, aye, Captain."

He pushed away from her with a grunt, not completely satisfied but confident he'd made his point.

****

Poppy released her stalled breath as Dakota turned to finish nailing the board he'd taken from her. The man certainly packed a solar plexus wallop, one she enjoyed just a tad too much. She wasn't sure what it was about his attitude that tempted her to push his buttons, only that she got a kick out of riling him. Maybe it was because she got bored easily and he was a challenge she hadn't undertaken before. The new job and location should have appeased her restlessness for a lot longer than the few weeks she'd lived in Idaho and worked for Jerry. Maybe she should have considered turning to more schooling instead of another job and new residence, her other go-to choice whenever the mood for something different had struck following the bone marrow failure.

Dakota unbuttoned his black work shirt and let the sides fall open to reveal his wide, thickly muscled smooth chest and rippling abs, and her first thought was, *nope, I'm right where I want to be at this moment.* She would love to wrap her arms and legs around that massive body and simply hold on for a rough ride, but, given his attitude toward her, that lustful desire would have to remain a fantasy. But, *wow*, what a dream to cling to for entertainment while she worked.

Discarding the nail gun, he bent over to pick up a hammer, the move stretching his jeans across his tight butt and showcasing his quads and hamstrings bulging against the snug denim. Poppy flicked her gaze toward his horse, the stallion as massive and dark as his master, and thought the two were made for each other. A large hand turned upside to reveal callouses she imagined scraping over her sensitive skin was thrust under her eyes.

"Nail."

"Oh, got it." She laid one on his palm, picturing those long fingers plucking at her nipples. Heat that had nothing to do with the afternoon sun shining down on her head enveloped her body. Either she was hornier than she'd thought, given the sexual drought caused by her illness, or she was coming down with something.

Poppy's pulse leaped as he swung the hammer and his forearm muscles, revealed by his rolled-up sleeves, bunched with each pound on the nail, and she imagined him braced on his arms as he loomed above her naked body. Door number one, definitely. Pure, unadulterated lust was the only thing that made sense.

Wanting to hear his deep, rumbling voice again, she put another nail in his outstretched hand, asking, "Did you grow up on the ranch?"

"Nope."

Okay. "Where did you grow up?"

"Arizona."

She cocked her head, regarding him with a frown as he made quick work of driving that nail into the wood then thrusting his arm out sideways for another one. "I've never been there. I'm from Houston, though, and used to warmer climates than here. These temps are nice for spring."

Dakota grunted again, his way of answering, she guessed. Even that sound managed to curl her toes, and she figured if this kept up, she would need to find a bed partner before long to take the edge off. It was either that or risk life and limb attempting to jump his bones. The thought produced a giggle, which prompted him to face her with an annoyed glare that – yep – sent another blast of heated awareness pumping through her veins.

"What?" she asked, pasting on an innocent expression.

"You tell me."

She shook her head. "You tell me what brought you here to Idaho. Family? A job? School?"

He stiffened and faced forward again to hammer in the next nail with extra force. "You writing a book?"

"No, at least not yet. That is on my list of careers to try, though. I think it would be fun. Want to be the model for my slutty romance novel?"

"Fuck, no."

Poppy laughed, loving his disgruntlement. Maybe she *was* getting sick.

Straightening, Dakota turned and said, "You're a pain in the ass, know that?"

"Yeah, I've heard it before. But not from anyone I cared about, so it didn't matter." She shrugged. "As long as my parents are happy with me, that's all that matters." Recalling her mother's stricken face after meeting Poppy's birth mother dampened her mood. She hated that her illness and *that* woman had caused her parents so much pain.

Dakota cocked his head, his gaze steady on her face. "Did you just think of something you did they didn't like?"

Talk about astute. Those black-as-night eyes, even shielded by his hat brim, missed nothing. Poppy returned his direct look with an indirect answer. "Nothing I did, but something to do with me, yes. Something out of all of our control. Are you almost done?"

Dakota took a disconcerting moment to reply,

as if trying to figure out what she'd omitted, before he said, "One more board, and that will finish this section."

She handed him another nail, wanting to rile him again simply because he caught her unaware with his considering gaze after that last comment. "So, do you have any hot friends who like skinny girls you can introduce me to?"

Exasperation colored his tone as he grunted. "Fuck, girl, would you just be quiet and let me finish this?"

Ooooh, he didn't care for that inquiry. Good to know. "Tsk, tsk, what would your mother say about that language."

Those broad shoulders went rigid then he blew out a rough breath and surprised her with an apology. "Sorry." Of course, he had to go and ruin it by adding, "Now, shut up."

Ten minutes later, Poppy jumped down from her perch on the rail and reached for the water bottle at her waist. Watching Dakota ride away, her mind still in the gutter, going over fantasies involving him and that sweaty, big body, she took a long drink to cool down. When the cold water failed to calm her overheated libido, it was her turn to swear and, pulling out her shirt, she poured the remaining water down her torso.

"*Ahhh*, much better." At least for now, and likely only until she happened to come across him again.

CHAPTER THREE

Poppy returned to the cabin and took a long shower, enjoying a few fantasies of sharing the small, wet cubicle with a naked Dakota as she ran her sudsy hands over her achy, sweaty body. She sighed with a shudder as she indulged in a pleasant tweak of her nipples, wishing she had the energy to play more. That light tug zapped her pussy with a quick lightning bolt of heat, but she wasn't up to anything more than a lingering wash between her legs. As much as she liked goading the hot neighbor, his disgruntled attitude could get tiresome. She knew better than most how short life could be, and not to waste a precious moment of it on anyone who didn't appreciate her time.

Still, she admitted, stepping out of the shower, she hadn't found anything else around here as entertaining as screwing with Dakota Smith. Maybe, if they happened to cross paths again, she would consider saying or doing something that would get a rise out of him, just for fun. Of course, if she thought she could get a different, more physical rise from him, such as an erection, she could get all over that.

She wasn't sure a return of her libido was a good thing, not if she couldn't meet someone to cut loose with for a while.

To take her mind off the gorgeous, copper-toned, dark-eyed neighbor and his bulging, sweat-slick muscles, Poppy fixed a quick sandwich for dinner and trekked over to have a chat with her boss. She knocked on the slider then opened it far enough to announce her arrival, not giving Jerry a chance to send her away.

"Hey, Jerry, I met your neighbor," she said as he came into the great room from the kitchen when he heard her.

Wearing his usual scowl, he fisted his hands on his hips as he halted in the middle of the room. "I told you to call me Sanders, hell, you can even call me Old Man Sanders for all I care. Why aren't you meeting me in my office?"

"Because in here is where your chess set is, and tonight works for me to get started on beating the pants off you. And, if you don't care, then I'll call you Jerry." She patted his shoulder as she strolled by him on her way to the table in front of the fireplace.

He eyed her askance then heaved a long-suffering sigh and joined her. Hiding a smile, Poppy sat in front of the white chess pieces, waiting for his next complaint.

Instead, he took the opposite seat and asked, "Which neighbor?"

"The very unhappy one because you didn't move on repairing the fence. Dakota Smith."

This time, he was the one smirking, only he didn't try to hide it from her. "He called. What did you think of him?"

Ah, so that was it. Jerry was well aware of Dakota's gruff personality. He should know by now Poppy wasn't put off by taciturn men, at least not at first. Eventually they would bore her, but after a year of everyone she cared about either tiptoeing around her or babying her due to her health, she found both men's honest surliness refreshing, and a challenge that had been lacking in her life for so long. She had gone into work when she could, but even when at her corporate management desk, she'd had to either struggle to stay focused because of the draining chemo treatments or had grown irritated with the pitying looks and consolatory comments from co-workers.

"I think he's a hunk I wouldn't mind getting to know better, and that he's as cranky as you but half the time doesn't mean it." She shifted a rook, satisfied with Jerry's frown at her accuracy. "Your move."

They played in silence for several minutes before he broke it with a comment she hadn't expected.

"Smith's an okay guy. Cooper did right by those boys."

"Those boys?" If Dakota had brothers, they might be worth checking out as potential partners in her quest to alleviate the increasing ache of lust plaguing her lately.

Sanders nodded without looking up from moving his knight into a position that had her pausing to think. "The Coopers took in three parentless teenage boys, none of them related, 'bout twenty years ago. Old Buck lived long enough to watch them grow into fine enough men to leave his spread to but still took care of Miss Betty, his wife." He glanced toward his wife's photo with a sad expression that tugged at Poppy's compassionate side then pleased her when he opened up just a crack to admit, "It's hard, losing a spouse."

"I imagine even harder when you don't have children. My birth mother dumped me as soon as I left her body, but I have awesome parents and can't imagine how difficult it must have been for Dakota and his friends to lose theirs."

Poppy almost grinned when her boss straightened with a scowl, as if realizing he'd let his usual crabbiness slip, and had revealed more than he'd intended. "Everyone has their difficulties. Why should they be any different? Be quiet and play or leave."

"I'll be quiet if you'll promise to get someone out here this week to finish the fence repairs."

He grunted, a sound of frustrated annoyance that reminded her of Dakota. "Fine, anything to get some peace and quiet from your nagging."

"You could always fire me," she returned, eyeing his aggressive move of his queen. "But then you'd have to find someone else, and you know as well as I, there are few who will put up with you."

"So, why do you?" he asked, looking at her with a touch of anger.

"Because I like it here, you're a challenge I won't give up on just yet, and you have a neighbor who entertains me. But fair warning, my tolerance will only go so far. Check."

"What the hell? Girl, would you please clam up now and let me concentrate?"

"Sure, Boss."

Jerry's phone call at the crack of dawn the next morning woke Poppy from a sound sleep and lovely dream that involved a large, male body wringing multiple orgasms out of her. For once, his grouchiness didn't amuse her.

"The contractor is on his way to work on the fences. You've got fifteen minutes before I send him over."

He hung up without another word, and she rolled out of bed with a groan, questioning her sanity in putting up with the old man. She would see the fences were all repaired today then inform Jerry she was taking the entire weekend off. He could just get his scraggly butt out to the pens and tend his own livestock for a change, and if not, well, he didn't know she would never leave him high and dry, without management help. The sheep deserved better.

By late afternoon, Poppy watched from her stance on the neighbor's side of the split rails as the last of the fence repairs were finished and the four workers took off in their truck. Satisfied with the job, she'd pushed away and started to climb over when the clop of an approaching rider made her pause. Turning her head, she eyed the blonde astride a petite mare veer her way and rein to a stop a few feet from Poppy.

"Hi there. Are you Old Man Sanders' new

manager?" she asked, dismounting and striding forward with a welcoming smile.

"I am." Holding out her hand, Poppy introduced herself. "Poppy Flynn."

"Lisa Halldor." She returned her handshake with a smile that lit up her green eyes. "I've been meaning to get over there and introduce myself but haven't had the time." Her eyes dimmed, her mouth tugging down in a sad expression before she seemed to rally from whatever thought had pulled her away for a moment. "Are you from around these parts?"

"No, Houston. You?" Leaning against the fence, Poppy regarded Lisa with interest in meeting a new friend. So far, the only people she'd connected with here were her boss and Dakota, and she wouldn't label either man as a friend.

Lisa joined her at the rail, her short-sleeved jade blouse tucked into jeans molded to fit a slender body Poppy tried not to envy.

"Phoenix, born and raised until recently. This sure is a change from hot and arid ten months out of the year. I can't say I'm looking forward to winter."

"Is there something, or someone, more enticing than a winter spent in a better climate?" Poppy doubted she would still be here come late fall, guessing either her health, the itch for something new or different, or the weather would prompt her to make another change.

"Oh yeah. The six-foot-two deputy sheriff who's part owner of this spread. I'm shacking up with him at his place, about two miles that way." She pointed south.

The blush staining Lisa's pale face that went with the small grin curling her lips spoke volumes. Poppy couldn't believe the stab of longing the other woman's pleased look caused her, a new and unwelcome feeling she quickly shoved aside. This was not the time in her life to wish for something like a relationship that lasted longer than a few weeks.

"It can't be the man I met, a drop-dead gorgeous hunk," she replied, thinking of Dakota.

Lisa gave her a curious look. "Why?"

Poppy's low laugh resonated between them. "Because he's the most uptight jerk I've ever met, and I figure he seriously needs to get laid."

A knowing, secretive look entered Lisa's eyes. "You're talking about Dakota. Trust me, getting laid isn't his problem. Once you get to know him, he lightens up."

She couldn't imagine that and shrugged. "I don't think he's interested in getting to know me better. But I'd like to meet your deputy sheriff. I haven't had a chance to meet many people yet."

"I know how hard that is as I've only been here a short time. I know!" Lisa's smile widened. "Can you join me for lunch in Mountain Bend tomorrow? Jen, my first friend here, and I are getting together at the deli."

Lunch out with friends – how long had it been since she'd done that or even wanted to? Poppy's appetite had only recently come back strong enough to eat three meals a day bigger than half a sandwich.

"I can, thank you," she replied, grateful for the invitation. "I'll meet you there and do a little shopping beforehand."

"Let's say noon." Lisa reached for her horse's reins. "Right now, I have to get back before Shawn comes looking for me."

A look of sadness came over her, but she turned away before Poppy caught more than a glimpse. "Protective, is he?" she asked as Lisa swung up into the saddle and sent her shoulder-length hair swinging. Poppy scooped back her short curls, remembering when her hair had been that long. In the months since her treatments had ended, there had only been time for it to grow long enough to frame her face and tickle her jaw.

"Yes, with good reason," Lisa answered,

settling on the saddle and gazing down at her. "See you tomorrow, Poppy."

"I'm looking forward to it." Poppy lifted her hand in a wave then hiked back to the cabin, tired but overall, quite pleased with the end of the week and looking forward to the weekend.

****

Dakota entered Spurs Friday night irked with himself and his shitty day. He wasn't used to a woman occupying his thoughts, and the fact it was the one who rubbed him wrong every time they met only added to his pissy mood. He had tried running through the long list of things about Poppy Flynn , and when that failed to do the trick, switched to going over her physical attributes. He'd stopped at two negatives, too skinny and short hair, unable to convince himself her small breasts and slender legs weren't among his preferences. Truth was, he'd always found favor with every body type and had never chosen a bed partner based on appearance.

He was later than usual tonight due to procrastinating while trying to come up with a good excuse to shirk his duties in maintaining their investment. If Shawn could return to pull his weight just two weeks after taking a bullet to protect his girl, he could damn well put in the time despite his lack of enthusiasm. Too bad the sucker after Lisa hadn't known who he was dealing with, and now never would. At least she was free of the bastard for good, even if his death weighed on her conscience. With luck, the return trip to Arizona Shawn was planning would settle the matter for her.

Entering from the foyer, Dakota noticed several couples already filled the small dance floor. He eyed two pairs of naked, bouncing breasts before taking in the scenes at the apparatus stations and had no trouble finding Clayton teasing a curvy brunette, her wrists bound above her on a dangling chain. With a snap of his hand and satisfied grin, he struck her pubis with the single-braid crop. From the way she arched and thrust her pelvis forward, Dakota assumed she had wanted that next strike to land on the sensitive flesh between her legs. Communication was key in such scenes, whether it was verbal or demonstrative, as long as they were adept at reading each other correctly.

Dakota's sweeping gaze landed on Shawn's pretty schoolteacher seated at the bar situated along the side of the enormous, renovated space. Since Shawn stood behind the mahogany bar top drawing a beer, he assumed his friend was taking over for Ben until Shawn's wound was completely healed. Striding that way, he nodded to a few members but didn't pause to talk. While he indulged in a spirited debate once in a while, he rarely had the patience to spend his limited downtime in idle chatter.

He gave Lisa's hair a friendly tug as he took the seat next to her. "You're looking better," he told her, noticing her green eyes were free of shadows tonight. He could imagine how difficult she found learning her stalker was a half-brother she never knew about.

"Everyone has been so supportive and understanding, which is helping. Plus, I have someone who's constantly around to keep me grounded." Her gaze softened as she looked at Shawn.

Shawn reached out and cupped her nape, drawing her forward over the bar for a quick kiss. "Remember that." He released her and turned to Dakota. "Father Joe says he hasn't heard from you in a while and wanted to know if you were coming for a visit when we go next month. We'll be done with spring planting by then."

"I've been busy, and someone has to stick around to run things." When Shawn just stared without backing down, Dakota gave in with a huff.

"Yeah, okay, I'll give him a call. But I *have* been swamped lately."

He wasn't opposed to staying in touch with the man whose intervention into his, Shawn's, and Clayton's lives turned out to be the best thing for them. But with Shawn now running for sheriff, on top of his duties as a deputy sheriff, and Clayton taking more and more cases from the overburdened Boise prosecutor's schedule, he wasn't comfortable leaving during the busier days of spring round-up and the start of crop growing. More work and longer days went hand in hand with warmer weather.

Lisa shifted her glance between Shawn and Dakota. "I met your neighbor's new sheep manager earlier. She seems nice, and I invited her to lunch tomorrow since you're working, Shawn."

"Our neighbor," Shawn corrected her.

"Hey, give me time to adjust, please. We only just moved in together." She looked up at Dakota. "Poppy mentioned already meeting you."

From her smirk, Dakota guessed Poppy didn't mince words over her impression of him, and damn it, why did she have to mention the irksome woman when he'd finally shoved her out of his head? He shrugged with indifference, determined to forget about her again. "She's okay but can get irritating."

Lisa and Shawn both laughed. "You find everyone annoying at some point," Shawn drawled. "How did those two leads pan out? Any luck?"

Dakota took the whiskey Shawn handed him and kicked back a healthy swallow, ignoring his first comment before answering his questions. "No. One wasn't living anywhere in the state at the time, and the other had just moved to Phoenix that month, not long enough to be the same Vincent coming around for almost a year." His mood was always lowest when a new lead in his mother's death didn't bear fruit. Twenty years was a long time to make good on his oath to avenge her, and he wouldn't stop until he kept that promise.

"I would say I'm sorry, but since I know what you're planning if you ever do find the man responsible for killing Wiyaka, I won't," Shawn returned.

Lisa frowned at him, and Dakota figured he hadn't gotten around to telling her about his mother's murder and his quest to take an eye for an eye.

"Shawn, why don't you support him? He's your friend."

"Which is precisely why I won't. He's seeking information about the man who murdered his mother so he can kill him. I would hate to have to testify against my friend, but I'm sworn to uphold all laws."

Lisa winced at hearing Dakota's plans, and he hated the guilt he felt knowing she was struggling with the death of the man who had tormented her. But, as fond as he'd become of her, no one would sway him from his course. "You won't have to. Do you honestly think I can't slip in and out of any house undetected?" Spending his early years on the reservation, getting picked on for being a half-breed, had taught him how to sneak around.

Master Simon hailed Shawn from the other end of the bar, and he clamped his mouth shut on whatever he'd been about to say, instead turning to Lisa. "Why don't you go visit with Charlotte until Clayton spells me?" He nodded toward a table, and Dakota saw their cute receptionist sitting alone.

"Good idea." Lisa patted his arm as she slid off the stool, her way of letting him know everything was good between them.

To lighten the air between them before Shawn walked away, Dakota said, "If Lisa had a sister, I might find myself tempted into trying more than a hookup, like you."

"I'll believe that if I see it, but you're right. It's

definitely not temporary between us, even if we're taking it slow, still getting to know each other. But when it's right, it's right, and you know it. Catch you later."

Dakota should feel bad he never volunteered for a shift behind the bar, but everyone agreed his less-than-congenial personality was a better fit for monitor and bouncer. And it was time he made himself useful and pulled his weight. Most nights, he enjoyed taking a walk around the renovated, two-story log building that dated back to the early 1900s and started as a saloon and brothel. A fire in '28 had gutted the inside, collapsing the upper floor. The next owner turned it into a warehouse and then it sat empty until the previous owner, Randy Daniels, had sunk a fortune into renovating instead of razing. Now, it was the only private club within a hundred miles. Glancing up, he noticed the doors to the rooms on the new second level they'd added were all closed, occupied with those guests who preferred privacy for their play.

Dakota didn't care either way, public or private, whatever the submissive needed as long as she didn't take his attention to mean anything more than a temporary Dom/sub scene. He stopped a moment to visit with another rancher before reaching Clayton, who had moved his sub to the fucking machine.

"She rides like a pro," Dakota commented, nodding toward the slow-rolling, padded vault and the woman lifting up and down on the attached, condom-covered phallus.

"Vicki is very agile, aren't you, sweetheart?" Clayton flicked his crop on her nipple, and she shuddered, biting her lower lip with a groan.

If Dakota went by the damp glistening of her labia clamped around the dildo, this one was into the sharp bite of pain. By this time, he was normally wound up enough to start scoping for a willing partner to approach after ending his rounds. But as he stood there, the image of Poppy sitting astride the apparatus, her slender body quaking as she gyrated on the vibrating toy, filled his head. With a low curse, he spun on his heel and stalked away, only to pass a chain station and imagine her arms stretched tautly above her head.

"Enough of this shit," he muttered, wondering why he couldn't put her out of his mind. For God's sake, he didn't even like the woman.

He took up residence against the far wall where he could keep an eye on everything. His face and crossed arms must reflect his displeasure because no one engaged him in conversation. The one girl who started his way, pivoted and walked in the opposite direction after getting close enough to read his mood. She wasn't the first he'd scared off, and wouldn't be the last, he admitted without a twinge of remorse.

And then Kathie headed his way, the perky troublemaker blonde having a way about her that endeared her to all the Doms, except him. He just tolerated her better than others. She was one of the few brave enough to take him on, liking his long spankings when she acted up, which she did often and on purpose. She was a harmless tease, always out for a good time and nothing else, and, in the past, he hadn't minded indulging her. Tonight, he did.

"Master Dakota." Kathie beamed at him, leaning close enough for him to see her full, bare breasts down her low-cut camisole. "I was hoping to catch you before you snagged someone else. I've been dying to try the new bench with you."

Dakota didn't mince words with her. "You should know by now flattery doesn't work with me. Go away, Kathie."

"Aww, don't be like that," she cajoled, running her fingers over his bare arm, below his rolled-up sleeve.

He might be an ass, but he was a fair ass, and it wouldn't be right to take her up on her offer in his current mood, not when his mind insisted on dwelling on a pale, skinny redhead. He plucked her hand off his arm and dropped it.

"Kathie, either scram or I'll call Master Simon over to punish you." He narrowed his eyes as she reddened, and her nipples puckered under the sheer white lingerie.

A mischievous gleam entered her eyes as she lifted her hand to caress his arm again. "I prefer you tonight, Master Dakota."

Okay, he was done playing nice. "Since you can't take no for an answer, or seem to obey my order"—he lifted her hand off him again, dousing her look of expectation—"you will refrain from participating with anyone tonight as punishment. Don't let me find out you've disobeyed that order."

Her mouth set in a mutinous pout, and in a rare show of anger, she stomped her small, bare foot and stormed off to join a few girls at a table. When they all looked his way with frowns, he could guess what she was telling them. Tired and annoyed with his thoughts, he decided to leave as soon as he could get Ben or Simon to take over. With luck, tomorrow night his mood would improve enough to take Kathie up on her offer.

An hour later, Dakota caught Ben as he sent his sub off with a satisfied glow and started toward the bar. The park ranger loved the outdoors and spent as much time outside as Dakota, which showed on his sun-darkened face. Like him, Ben was used to leaving his hat on more than off out of habit when inside.

"Hey, how's it going tonight?"

Dakota shook his head. "Tiresome, for some reason. Can you take over monitoring the last hour?"

"We all have nights like that. No problem. Now, can I ask you a favor?" He fisted his hands on his hips and blew out a breath of disgust. "I've found evidence that grizzly is wounded, likely in bad shape. Which fucking pisses me off. Damn hunters need to be more careful."

"I hear you." Hunting for sport and eating the meat instead of letting the carcasses rot was all good and well, but it was cruel not to aim to kill, or to neglect finishing what they started by letting a wounded animal get away. "If you want help tracking him, let me know." Since he was the best tracker around these parts, Dakota often volunteered for hunts.

"Thanks. I appreciate the offer and will take you

up on it if the park staff fails to find him soon. If he is injured, given the time frame, my guess is a minor wound has worsened and infected. I'm holding out hope he passes on his own, or it's something else altogether."

"If it's unexplainable causes for his rampage, that puts people at a higher risk. Don't hesitate to enlist not only my help but Shawn and Clayton's. Thanks for spelling me tonight."

****

Poppy drove into Mountain Bend Saturday morning an hour before she was supposed to meet Lisa at the deli. She didn't like the fact she couldn't stop thinking about Dakota, even if she enjoyed the late-night fantasies disturbing her sleep. She hadn't slept a night through since undergoing chemo, and, unlike the return of her appetite, the ability to do so remained absent. The perspiration-inducing, pussy-cramping side effects of those dreams were worth the physical torment and kept her mind off other, less desirable matters. Such as fretting over a return of her cancer or going through another rejected bone-marrow transplant.

The odds of her surviving a return of this

disease were still good, but knowing that, and what she'd have to go through again, made remaining optimistic sometimes difficult, especially when she looked in the mirror and saw the lingering ravages from the chemicals. She was still down twelve pounds, and her stamina remained low, but she was getting there and was proud of how far she'd driven herself to recover all she'd lost already.

After parking in front of the deli, she took her time visiting the shops on that street and one over, on Main. It had been so long since she'd indulged in a frivolous shopping spree. She opened the door to the candle shop, inhaling the pleasant scents before noticing the older woman in the corner, standing by a large double broiler on a small cooktop. She hadn't expected to see candle making in process. The woman looked over and waved for her to browse.

"Have a look-see, dear, and I'll be right with you. Are you wanting a particular fragrance?"

"I'm not picky, but something strong enough to dispel the musty odor of an old cabin." Opening the windows hadn't helped rid her cabin of its woodsy, closed-up smell.

"Oh, you must be Old Man Sanders' new manager. He shouldn't have put you in that cabin, but knowing him, he likely wanted you away from the house." She shook her head and removed the broiler from the heat before padding to the shelves Poppy had stopped in front of. "Here." Plucking down a cute mason jar holding a white candle, she held it out to Poppy. "Vanilla bean, my best seller. Let's add a sweet mulberry, too, just for variety."

Poppy took a whiff of each. "These are perfect. Thank you." Before she was tempted to check out a few more fragrances and then have to decide between them, she followed the owner to the counter, handing over cash after the proprietress rang up the total.

The woman surprised Poppy by grabbing her fingers and examining her ragged nails with a concerned frown. "Oh my, girl. Look at those nails, bitten to the quick. And you have such lovely hands."

Poppy didn't bother telling her they were brittle due to the drugs, instead, gently pulling her hand away. "I have trouble keeping them in shape."

"You mosey down to Cee Cee's on the corner. Tell her Anna Lee sent you. She has a nail hardener that'll fix you right up. I get it applied once a month, and it works wonders." Anna waved her shiny, manicured nails.

"Thank you, Anna Lee, I'll do that," she agreed after seeing proof of Cee Cee's work.

Anna shook a finger at Poppy. "And don't let

that man run you off. Stand up to him. Just because he lost his wife, God rest her soul, is no excuse for him to be such a grouch all the time."

Tickled by her attitude, so similar to Poppy's, she smiled. "Don't worry, I decided that on day one. We're playing chess every evening now, and he's loosening up."

"*Ooooh*, you go, girl. Don't be a stranger, now."

"I'll be back, since I intend to burn these nonstop. Nice to meet you."

Dropping Anna Lee's name at the beauty shop worked, and since Cee Cee was in between appointments, she promptly seated Poppy at the small manicure table and talked nonstop gossip for the next thirty minutes, bobbing her bleached, blue-streaked hair for emphasis. By the time she finished, her nails were smooth and shiny, the clear coating making a vast improvement, and she'd heard about Chester Campbell's frequent abuse of his wife, Louise, and their nosy neighbor, Gladys Archibald. Kevin, one of the deputy sheriffs, had been dating Susan Marie for six years, since high school, and she was getting tired of waiting for a proposal. The Whitcombs welcomed their third grandchild this week, and Lori Tavers just announced her first pregnancy.

Poppy managed to squeeze in a few words about meeting Lisa for lunch, but that was all.

"This one is on the house, sweetie," Cee Cee said as two women entered the salon and Poppy stood, reaching for her purse.

"But you did such a beautiful job. Are you sure?"

"Don't argue with Cee Cee," one of the newcomers called out. "Won't do you any good."

"Listen to them and enjoy your lunch. I have yet to meet Deputy Sheriff Shawn's girl, but I've seen her with him. Adorable couple. We're all grateful our good deputy, along with a few of his cowhands, saved her from that horrible man."

Unlike the rest of the gossip, Poppy couldn't wait to hear that whole story. As soon as she entered the deli, she smelled fresh-baked homemade bread, and her stomach rumbled. There was a line in front of the counter, and all the meat and cheese choices displayed in the case. Spotting Lisa sitting with another woman at a corner table, she veered that way, looking forward to meeting her friend, and to hearing the rest of Lisa's story.

Taking the empty seat, she let her curiosity rip without thinking. "Before I start drooling over homemade bread, fill me in. Your deputy boyfriend and some cowboys saved you from a crazy person? Tell me. Inquiring minds want to know more about that than the love lives of Mountain Bend's citizens and every baby born this past week."

"I'm Jen, and I'm guessing you just came from Cee Cee's." Jen held her hand out across the small, round table.

Poppy clasped her hand. "Poppy Flynn. If Cee Cee is the town gossip, she's a delightful one. Is she always that forthcoming or just with newcomers?"

"Always." Jen sent Lisa a concerned look, and Poppy realized her blunder.

"I'm sorry, Lisa. I popped off without thinking. If it bothers you, forget I said anything." Poppy breathed a sigh of relief when Lisa smiled.

"No, no, it's fine. I can't help but feel guilty because a man lost his life. That's what bothers me. For months, I suffered him stalking me without knowing who he was or why he focused on me. Turns out, the father I never knew raised his son to covet money more than people. It's sad all the way around."

Lisa was a better person than her. Poppy didn't think she would suffer such guilt if it had been her. "Yeah, I guess, but I doubt I'd be as sympathetic as you."

"Me, either," Jen admitted. "Let's talk about you, Poppy. What brought you to Mountain Bend? Surely Old Man Sanders and his sheep weren't the only reasons for your move."

Poppy thought a moment before answering. Lisa hadn't hesitated to talk about her recent ordeal, and, if she wanted to cultivate these friendships, she should return the open honesty.

"If it's personal, don't fret. I understand better than you think," Lisa said.

"No, not that personal. I was coming off months of chemo treatments and bone marrow rejections and wanted to get away for a while. I found the job opening, have an unused degree in animal husbandry, and took it as a positive sign. And, yes, I'm cancer-free right now, with a good prognosis that will get better if I manage a successful transplant. In the meantime, I'm working on gaining my health back, so what do you recommend?"

"We can help with that." Jen rattled off her favorite sandwiches then said, "I'm going for the messy meatball sub today."

"I'm partial to the spicy Italian," Lisa added. "And if you're hungry for a big meal, Jen's B&B has the best Sunday brunch."

"I'll be there tomorrow if you'll give me

directions. Today is my treat. Be right back." She left the table before they could protest and got in line at the counter. Within a few minutes, she was carrying a tray with three foot-long sandwiches, chips, and iced teas, her ears perking up as she got close enough to hear Lisa mention a club.

"There's a club around here? Closer than Boise?" she asked, setting the tray down. "I haven't been out in ages." Jen and Lisa exchanged a wary glance, but Poppy didn't care if she'd come across as pathetic or pushy, as she didn't mind going alone. "I won't intrude on your plans. I went clubbing by myself often in Houston," she said, resuming her seat and reaching for her sandwich.

"No, sorry, it's not that at all, Poppy."

Lisa hedged again, tweaking her curiosity until Jen picked up for her and explained.

"Spurs isn't a public club, Poppy. And it's not only for socializing."

"Huh?" Then a lightbulb went off, and Poppy understood. Amusement mixed with a ripple of excitement shot through her. Leaning forward, she whispered across the table. "A kink club? Do they allow ogling visitors?"

"Seriously? You want a visitor's pass?" Lisa's eyes sparkled with humor. "Because I happen to know one of the owners."

Jen grinned. "Lisa's sleeping with one of the owners."

"Your deputy owns a kink club? Does that mean Dakota is also a member and part-owner?" It would make sense since the two owned a ranch together and were close friends. Screwing with Dakota had entertained her since arriving here, and even though that sexual lifestyle had never interested her, she did think it would be fun to check the place out, and his reaction to seeing her there.

"You have an interest in BDSM?" Lisa asked quietly.

Poppy snorted. "No. I can never see me saying *yes, sir* to any man other than a boss, out of respect. But who wouldn't like watching, at least once? If that's allowed. I don't want to put you on the spot with your deputy."

"You're not. Let me see what I can do. It'll be fun having you there and witnessing your reaction."

Poppy already knew what her reaction would be – indifference. It was Dakota's she was looking forward to seeing the most.

CHAPTER FOUR

Poppy followed Lisa's directions later that evening and found Spurs without difficulty. As she pulled into the crowded parking area in front of the log structure, she began second-guessing her decision to meet Lisa inside instead of taking her up on her offer of a ride with her and the deputy. At the time, she thought it would be easier to leave when she was ready if she didn't have to rely on transportation from someone else. There was no telling how long she would hang around, given her lack of interest in anything the club offered except a chance to get under Dakota's skin again.

Several people entered while she sat there, and she eyed the hip-hugging skirts and shorts on the women, hoping her just-above-the-knee, simple sheath passed the dress code Lisa mentioned. One man wore black leathers and a matching vest that revealed the thick, sculpted muscles of his chest. Sexy as hell, especially with his bald head and the heated look he gave the two women he held the door open for. Her imagination was already running amok as she slid out of her vehicle.

The nights here in Idaho were much cooler than in Texas this time of year, and, as she closed the door, she shivered from the slight breeze brushing her bare arms and legs. With a brisk step, and before she caved to questioning her sanity in deciding to come here, she hightailed it across the lot and dashed inside, entering a large foyer. The bald man turned, eyeing her with an interest that heated Poppy's blood as the two women stored their shoes in small cubbyholes. It had been a long time since a man had leveled any attention on her, and since she was only human, and female, she basked in his slow appraisal.

"You must be our guest for tonight that Shawn mentioned a short time ago. Come on in. I'm Master Simon."

"Poppy Flynn. Thank you."

At least he didn't insist I address him as sir, she mused as he opened another door and waved her inside a cavernous room resonating with music, low voices, and sounds she couldn't name but that caused a shudder to ripple down her spine. Master Simon noticed and gave her a slow grin.

"You really are green, aren't you? Did you even research before coming here?"

Poppy shook her head, glancing around the

space, seeing some things that were quite titillating and others that turned her cold. "This is just a one-time visit." She left it at that when she spied Lisa heading her way, a tall good-looking man with a loose-limbed stride and wearing a black Stetson keeping a possessive hold of her hand.

"Master Simon, thank you for greeting my friend," Lisa said. "Poppy, this is Shawn." She smiled up at Shawn, and Poppy saw him squeeze her fingers before turning his full attention on her.

"Welcome to Spurs, Poppy. Would you like a tour or to sit and visit first?"

She could see why Lisa had fallen for the deputy sheriff. His voice alone could curl toes. Add in the whole package of rugged male, and the heart couldn't help but speed up a notch. "Going by what I can see from here, I think I better sit down first."

Simon chuckled and walked off as Shawn nudged his hat up enough to reveal his intent, gray eyes, his dark-mahogany hair curling around his nape and strong, tanned throat. "Why don't I get you two a drink and leave you alone for a spell. Poppy, what do you prefer?"

"A rum and coke, please. Here." She reached into her purse, but he shook his head.

"It's on the house, part of your guest pass. Grab

a table, and I'll be right back."

Lisa sighed, watching him walk toward the bar. "He's always so good at reading people. Come on. You must have a million questions."

"Oh, I think this might be a place where a scene speaks a thousand words." Taking a seat across from Lisa, Poppy commented with a raised brow, "I can see why you went for your deputy."

"You could say he grabbed me at hello, only our first meeting was over twenty years ago. He left such an impact on me as a kid, I never forgot him."

Intrigued, Poppy resisted the temptation to take a closer look at what was going on at a nearby padded bench to say, "Don't stop there. That would be mean. Tell me more, please."

"It was only a few hours, but that's all it took." Lisa revealed how the three teenage boys fled their abusive foster home one night, Shawn taking the time to rescue her from their stepfather's assault to carry her out with them.

"So, Dakota, the one I met on the ranch, he was part of this trio?"

"Yes, he and Clayton and Shawn were relocated to the Rolling Hills Ranch. Clayton is the local prosecutor." Lisa glanced around the room then pointed toward the back. "That's him at the St.

Andrew's Cross, with the sandy hair. I think the girl he's having fun with is Ella, but don't quote me on that."

"She can as you're correct," Shawn said as he set their drinks down. "Ella is one of the new members. Come get me at the bar when you're done here."

He bent and kissed Lisa long enough, and thoroughly enough, to cause a knot of envy to form in Poppy's stomach. She wasn't proud of that petty reaction and shifted her gaze to the row of apparatus, some of which appeared more tortuous than pleasurable. It still baffled her how anyone could get off by allowing their partner full control over their bodies and their responses.

"You have to try it to understand."

Lisa's amused comment drew her attention off the busty blonde draped over a man's lap, her buttocks a bright red from his spanking. "Letting some guy spank me like a misbehaving kid? I don't think I can get into that." Still, there was something about the girl's relaxed posture and the way she wiggled her hips with a small lift, as if begging for more, that stirred Poppy's curiosity. She couldn't deny watching the man caress the flesh he'd just abused with soft, soothing strokes was a bit of a turn-on, enough of one to dampen her panties.

"I can explain each piece, if you want to walk around."

"You've been at this awhile?" It was hard to picture her new, petite friend in such a role.

"About two years now, after my previous relationships failed in more ways than one. It surprised me, how easy it was to fall into the lifestyle, and even more, to reap the benefits once I submitted to Shawn. The right person can make all the difference for those who aren't out for just a good time."

"How about for those who are, like me? I'm thinking voyeurism is going to be the extent of my kink." There was no denying the arousing appeal of ogling others.

Lisa shrugged, the move lifting her satin spaghetti-strap top. "Hey, if that's your thing, go for it. Everything consensual is accepted. Want a closer look?"

"Yes, but I hope you'll understand if I say I prefer gawking on my own. This could get embarrassing, and I don't embarrass easily." Poppy gave her a rueful grin, hoping Lisa wasn't offended after inviting her tonight.

"Not at all, go ahead. I'll be at the bar with Shawn if you need anything. Everyone's nice, but be sure you don't interrupt a scene by talking to either participant, and show respect to the Doms. Guest or not, some things they won't let slide," she warned.

"In other words, keep my mouth shut," Poppy drawled, pushing to her feet.

Lisa giggled. "To play it safe, yeah. If you get adventurous, I'll join you in the hot tub out back when you're done."

"Now, that I can get into. Thanks. Catch you later."

Poppy wanted to ask about Dakota since she hadn't caught sight of him anywhere but refrained. If he didn't show up, she would still have a good time without the added perk of seeing her presence get under his skin. That proved true as she took her time strolling the loop around the cavernous room, pausing at each odd contraption, and staying long enough to first figure it out, and second to garner the reactions of the person bound on it. Those with a submissive side all possessed one thing in common – a satisfied, almost contented expression by the time their dominant partner assisted them out of bondage.

A strange longing swept over Poppy as she eyed another brawny, good-looking cowboy enfolding the naked, quivering form of a girl who collapsed in his arms when he released her cuffed wrists from a dangling chain. Her pale skin bore faint pink stripes from a wicked-looking narrow strap the man had returned to his waist. Poppy held her breath as he ran his fingers over the puffy red lines marring the girl's lower back and buttocks. Instead of yelping in discomfort, she shuddered and pressed closer to his muscled body with a sigh, her eyes closed and a small tilt to her lips that put a whole different spin on the kink.

Poppy still didn't think this was her cup of tea, but *damn*, there was no denying the draw for some, and the obvious mental relief that seemed to go hand in hand with the physical. Now, if one of these hunks wanted to bend her over and have his way with her, she just might add exhibitionism to kinks. Watching had definitely gotten her worked up to a higher, hotter degree than she'd enjoyed in an exceptionally long time.

When the ebony-haired man lifted his head from murmuring to the girl and turned bright-green eyes on her in a probing stare, she stumbled back a step, right into a tall, rock-hard muscled wall. The man in front of her grinned as a copper-toned thick arm slid around her waist, pinning her in place.

"Who do you have there, Master Dakota?"

Green Eyes asked.

"She's a pest, so you might want to stay clear, Ben."

Poppy stiffened and pulled out of Dakota's hold, surprised, and a touch disappointed he released her so fast. Annoyed with him, herself, and her instantaneous, combustible reaction to his sudden presence, she placed her fists on her hips, turned, and snapped, "I resent that, Dakota. Unlike you, Ben might like skinny redheads." *Oh shit.* He wore buckskin, thigh-molding pants and a brown leather vest, his bare, hairless chest a beacon for her eyes, itchy fingers, and aching nipples.

His brows lowered in a thunderous frown, and she fought back a grin. Even practically drooling with lust from all that tanned, smooth skin stretched over bulging muscles, she found herself amused that her mere presence here caused him grief. She took that as a sign she got under his skin in a way he wasn't prepared for or knew how to deal with. Much the same as she felt about him.

"I'm sure Lisa mentioned respect to you."

"*Ooops*, yes she did." She shrugged, unconcerned despite the gasp from the much-younger girl still leaning against Ben. "I forgot. How did you know Lisa invited me?"

"I've been here awhile," was all he said by way of explanation, but it was enough to produce a warm, fuzzy feeling in Poppy's abdomen.

"I'll leave you two alone. We're done here if you want this station." Ben nodded then led his partner toward a small sofa in a seating area and pulled her onto his lap, his fingers delving between the girl's thighs as soon as she spread them.

"What the hell are you doing here, Poppy? There's no way you're interested in what this club offers."

She dragged her eyes away from the unabashed couple to look up at him with a wicked grin. "You mean kink?"

"Yes," he ground out, towering over her, those coal-black eyes lingering on her pert nipples pressing against the thin silk of her sheath.

"Well, considering I'm all hot and bothered from watching, I think it's safe to admit I enjoy that much." Unable to help herself, she leaned into him, her blood warming from the sucked-in breath that lifted his pecs and his body heat penetrating her dress. She pressed her hands against his chest, the rapid beat of his heart against her palm another positive sign. "Tell me what you like here."

A calculating gleam entered his eyes, and just as

an *uh oh* popped into her head, he gripped a handful of the short curls at her nape and drew her face up to meet his descending mouth. "I'll show you instead."

As soon as Dakota's lips took control of hers, Poppy's thoughts went as haywire as her out-of-whack pulse. *Whoa! Attention all kinky sex shoppers. He-man assault on a pair of unsuspecting lips – aisle three.* She would have laughed, except his tongue took command of hers next. The aggressive strokes and glide of his mouth over hers robbed her of sanity. He worked his free hand between them, clasped one wrist, and drew it behind her to hold in a tight grip against her lower back.

Poppy lost all sense of awareness of those around her as she basked in the first, overwhelming body-sweep of sensation she could remember experiencing. Maybe the long sexual drought had caused her to forget some of her most memorable sex capades at that moment, or maybe nothing she'd done before compared to this kiss, or this man. Whatever the reason, his control as she tugged on her imprisoned wrist left her as shaken as the girl in chains who'd been put through a lot more than a kiss.

"*Wow,*" she breathed against his damp lips as he released her and pulled away. "When you put it that way, maybe I can get into this stuff."

Dakota blew out a breath, lifted his Stetson, and tunneled his fingers through his shoulder-length hair before lowering it again. "You're impossible, and because you are, I'm not turning you loose on my unsuspecting members. What haven't you checked out yet?"

Since she didn't mind spending more time with him in the least, Poppy didn't take umbrage at his high-handedness. First, she couldn't keep from needling him again. "You say the sweetest things. Admit it," she cajoled, batting her eyes and running a finger over his nipple until it puckered. "You like me."

"About as much as Phantom likes a burr under the saddle," he returned with a wry twist to his lips, but Poppy caught the slight thawing of his rigid expression. That was good enough for her to agree.

"I haven't made it to the other side yet."

Clasping her elbow, Dakota steered her that way, and Poppy wondered at the stab of disappointment because he hadn't taken her hand instead. She shoved aside that strange reaction to concentrate on enjoying his closeness and the deep rumble of his voice as they stopped at the third padded bench she'd seen, each different. This one left nothing to a viewer's imagination as she eyed the woman bound on her elbows and knees, her head and torso lower than her elevated hips.

"You can't be shy in here, can you?" she quipped, sneaking a glance at his expression. Instead of ogling the woman's gaping pussy and spread buttocks that revealed her plugged anus, his gaze focused on her. "What?" she asked, growing uncomfortable.

"Not a whole lot fazes you, does it?"

You do. "Oh, you'd be surprised, Mr. Smith."

"Master Dakota while here," was all he said before nodding to Simon, the man who had escorted Poppy inside and now turned from lifting a paddle off the wall of instruments.

"Okay," she agreed absently, her imagination spinning in all kinds of directions from contemplating the vast array of spanking implements.

"See something you want to try?" Simon asked her, running the leather side of the wooden paddle over his partner's clenching buttocks.

"Not in this lifetime." When both men glared at her, she rolled her eyes and drawled with exaggerated sarcasm, "Sir."

"A challenge for you, Master Dakota."

"Just what I need," he answered, his mocking tone matching hers.

"No, no challenge," Poppy stuttered on a laugh as Dakota nudged her forward, the flesh-smacking snap of Simon's swat echoing behind them.

"And here I took you for someone open to trying anything once."

In most cases, yes, and she thrived on challenges, but spanking? Nope, she couldn't picture herself going there, despite her piqued interest. But she did get a kick out of poking Dakota and leaned into him with a flirting grin. "Do you want to spank me, *Master* Dakota?"

The first full-fledged smile she'd gotten from him spread across his face, changing him from eye-drawing good-looking to knee-buckling devastating. *Be still my heart*. She groaned, struggling to get herself under control. Her heart was the last organ she wanted to involve when she thought of Dakota.

Instead of frowning, like she'd hoped, his smile reached his dark eyes. "Darlin', you have no idea. Tread carefully." Then he seemed to realize what he'd said, and to whom, because he stiffened with a shake of his head.

Warm tingles ghosted across Poppy's buttocks and tickled her pussy, instigated by his endearment and admission, then cooled and faded as he pivoted and led her to the padded wooden cross. She regretted the loss of that unexpected, titillating thrill then zeroed in on the threesome crowded together on a two-seat sofa instead of listening to Dakota's explanation of the restraints on the empty cross. Nothing she'd seen tonight had aroused her as much as one glimpse of the girl squished between two much larger men, her demi bra hanging open to reveal full, hard-tipped breasts, her short skirt rucked up to her waist, her legs spread over the men's thighs. Without panties, her damp pleasure in their attention was obvious to onlookers.

"Oh, yes," Poppy whispered as one man dipped his head to suck on a straining nipple and the other burrowed more than one finger between her glistening folds. She didn't realize she'd spoken aloud until Dakota shifted her in front of him, her back to his chest, and banded an arm across her lower abdomen.

"So, you finally found something that interests you."

"Newsflash, Dakota, there isn't a female breathing who hasn't fantasized about two men." Even with that hot image in her head and in front of her, the slow burn traveling through her bloodstream stemmed from his semi-erection pressed against her butt and his arm once again wrapped around her, holding her tight.

"That may be true, but few are brave enough to dive into the challenge. Are you?"

"Maybe." If he was one of the men involved. She didn't go so far as to say that out loud. "Never know until you try, right?"

Dakota took her elbow again and drew her past the busy trio toward the bar. "You would do best to start with mild restraint in public before jumping into an intense scene such as a ménage. Lisa is waving you over."

Poppy hadn't noticed but greeted her friend's interruption with relief. She needed a reprieve from her conflicting thoughts and emotions surrounding Dakota.

"She mentioned trying out the hot tub, which sounds pretty good about now."

The last time she'd dared to strip in front of others had been at a lakeside graduation party when the girls' tops and bras had come off, and she'd known a lot of those people. Getting naked outside and slipping into a large, swirling tub with strangers catching a peek from inside wouldn't bother her, and at least the high sides and water would disguise her less-than-desirable, still-too-thin body.

"Have fun, and, Poppy, behave, even if your

visit tonight is just for kicks."

She watched him stalk off right before they reached Lisa, thinking the evening might have started out that way, but her achy, throbbing girly parts were now saying something different. She was afraid to admit she might want more from the attitude-riddled neighboring rancher than she'd bargained for.

****

Dakota managed to fend off the urge to spin around and watch Poppy as she walked toward the back with Lisa. None of their encounters before tonight had prepared him for the hard kick to his groin when he'd spotted her bright-red head across the room. Stifling the compulsion to storm over and demand to know why she was here, as well as the unwanted spark of lust that had hit him, he'd kept an eye on her from a distance. Until he'd seen the look of avid interest and curiosity on her face as she'd watched Ben comfort Charlotte.

There had been something on her face, noticeable even from his short distance away, that had compelled him forward for closer perusal. *Longing.* That's what he'd glimpsed reflected on her face and in her expressive blue eyes when he'd walked close enough. While he could commiserate with often wanting more from life than ending a long day of work to continue a seemingly eternal search for his mother's murderer, he kept it buried under his determination to see the man paid. It had been easy, maybe too easy, to offer to finish Poppy's tour with her. His excuse of wanting her gone from the club had rung hollow in his mind, and he wouldn't act such an ass as to deny he'd liked witnessing the myriad emotions crossing her face and trading barbs with her. He found her open honesty refreshing, as there were always those irritating guests who visited for kicks and disdained everything they surveyed.

Poppy denied any interest in the lifestyle but hadn't put down those around her for their preferences. Instead, her looks reflected hints of respect and a touch of admiration, and she hadn't shied away from admitting she could be lured into trying a ménage. He didn't want to like anything about her, but damn, those traits appealed to him.

Dakota waited until Poppy and Lisa had time to stroll outside, presumably to get in the hot tub, before winding his way to the bar. They kept the lighting dim, but he could still get as clear a view of each bondage station from the bar as the other side of the room, and he could go for a cold brew about now. Clayton entered Spurs as Dakota passed the front doors, and he paused until Clayton joined him.

"Long day?" he asked, noticing Clayton's tired eyes.

"Too damn long for a Saturday. Our case load is backed up, so I had to schedule depositions today then attend an obligatory dinner with the DA and Boise staff. Fuck, but I hate politics." Clayton flashed a smile, dropping his disgruntled mood just that quick. "I'll have a beer with you, then I'm going to find a willing, needy sub to put through her paces."

"That'll make you feel better," he stated as they fell into step together.

"You bet. Anything going on tonight?" Clayton scanned the room with interest as they made their way to the bar.

"No, everything's gone without a hitch." Except for one feisty redhead Dakota was trying to keep his eyes off and his head clear from thinking about. Clayton enjoyed indulging his partners with a ménage. Maybe he should introduce Poppy to his friend. That ought to squelch her interest in him and satisfy her curiosity about a threesome.

He'd give it some thought as soon as his gut quit cramping.

"Lisa says you met Poppy before tonight." Shawn handed him and Clayton a beer as they settled on barstools.

"Sanders' sheep were on our property again." Dakota left it at that, not ready to discuss Poppy with either of them. The unaccustomed tug he'd experienced as he observed her reactions to the scenes needed to be examined, dealt with then shoved aside before he could answer too many questions about their acquaintance.

"That's what Rick said. Lisa likes her." Shawn shifted his gaze toward the glass doors.

"That's Poppy? The redhead?" Clayton whistled. "Nice butt."

Dakota whipped his head around, losing the battle to keep his eyes off her with Clayton's comment. And he was right, damn it – she did have a nice ass. She lifted one long leg over the tub's edge then the other, offering a nice view of her heart-shaped backside before turning around and sinking into the deep, steaming water. Her small breasts floated on top as she laid her arms along the shoulder-high decking behind her and leaned her head back. His cock thickened as he pictured those legs wrapped round his pumping hips, that image and his quick blood rush south spelling out clearly what he needed to do to get her out of his head.

He would offer a taste of the kink she claimed to have no interest in, settling the matter for both of them tonight so she could set her sights on a vanilla someone, and he could forget about her. The same as he'd done with every other woman.

He downed his beer and handed the bottle back to Shawn. "Excuse me." With luck, Poppy would balk at agreeing to anything he suggested, and he could end this before it went any further. With his priorities set in stone, there was no room in his life, or even time to contemplate why she bugged him and drew his curiosity all at once.

"Hold up, Dakota. I'm ready for a break myself. Clayton, do you mind?" Shawn jerked a thumb behind the bar.

"Not at all. You two go, have fun. Let me know if I can help with either one."

Clayton's suggestive grin was meant to get a rise out of over-possessive Shawn, and, Dakota suspected, to test him and his interest in Poppy. Clayton liked pushing their buttons as much as Poppy seemed to enjoy taunting him.

"In your dreams, Trebek," Shawn shot back while he and Clayton traded places behind the bar.

Dakota tossed out a different answer to Clayton.

"If I don't scare Poppy off, I may take you up on that."

He doubted Poppy could give up control to one man, let alone two, and acting on a fantasy was way different than admitting to an interest. Then again, she and Clayton would make a good match as neither took much seriously.

"You know where to find me," Clayton replied.

Dakota nodded then pivoted toward the rear doors, second-thinking that idea with a return of his stomach cramp. It might be best if she got interested in someone he wasn't in close contact with on a daily basis. Out of sight, out of mind would surely work in this case.

Shawn gave him a wary, somewhat reproachful glance as they reached the glass slider. "You seem more put upon than interested in whatever you have planned."

"I'm both." Dakota grabbed the door handle, his tone cool as he said, "Timid ones may run from me, but I've never harmed a woman, anywhere."

"And I didn't think you would start now, but she's a guest, one who's not really interested in the lifestyle. I'm just making sure you remember that."

"I do, and intend to remind her of it, that's all."

Stepping outside, the cooler air did nothing to temper his body heat as Dakota took in the closer view of Poppy's flushed face and pert, pink nipples, her pale shoulders, and chest damp from the bubbling water. As he strode forward to stand at the hot tub and look down at both girls, he couldn't pull his eyes off Poppy's slender body, bare beneath the swirling water, her long legs slowly gliding back and forth, slightly parted to reveal a tantalizing pink swath of her pussy. Hell, why did he have to be such a sucker for a bare, plump labia?

He tipped his hat back and cocked his head as Shawn lifted Lisa from the tub and Poppy didn't try to shield herself from either of them. "You're not shy even naked."

A mischievous smile curled her soft lips, and she shrugged one shoulder. "When in Rome, and all that. Are you going to join me?" Her gaze shifted to Shawn and Lisa as he hoisted her over his shoulder, and Lisa lifted her dangling head to give Poppy a finger wave.

"Catch you later, Poppy."

"Have fun," she called back as they returned inside. "Well?" she asked, looking back up at Dakota and running one hand through the water in invitation.

"No, I have a better idea." And one he needed to instigate fast, before he caved to his baser urges and got in to place her spread legs over his lap and lower her onto his cock. He took advantage of her position, which she hadn't changed, and reached along the side of the tub to pull up the restraint hidden there. "How about a mild taste of bondage, and giving up control?"

Poppy twisted her torso and head, her eyes widening as she took in the wrist cuff, her fingers curling into a fist as he watched her struggle with the challenge he'd just tossed out.

"Like you said earlier, you never know until you try. Or would you rather call it a night, and tell yourself you satisfied your curiosity about our place and what it offers?"

"I never said I was curious about bondage, but I'll play your game." Lifting her arm at the elbow, she wiggled her hand. "Go ahead."

Wrapping the cuff around her small wrist, he kept one eye on her face, watching for discomfort. "Say red when you want loose." She wouldn't panic, like some newbies, so the most he could hope for was a fast end to her bravado, or boredom, or plain dislike of the restraint.

Poppy tugged on her bound arm, her breathing hitching a notch, her slim, auburn brows dipping in a frown. Instead of insisting he release her, a bemused expression spread across her face. "Huh. That's not so bad, but I still don't know what the big deal is."

Great. Now, instead of wanting her gone, all he wished was to show her the benefits of turning herself and her pleasure over to a Dom. He supposed it had been too much to hope she would react the way he expected for once. "Does that mean you want to continue, or to end this?"

"Let's continue. This may be fun after all."

"Remember," he warned, sitting on the edge and leaning over, "you asked for this."

****

Poppy held her breath as Dakota's shoulder brushed hers when he reached into the hot water. She'd thought the zing his hold on her hair and wrist had given her earlier had stemmed from his touch, not her inability to move her head or arm. Now, she wasn't so sure, not after experiencing the same electric zap when she'd yanked on the wristband. Of course, having those obsidian eyes on her bare breasts and scanning below the water could also account for the hot flash. She wasn't about to call it a night without finding out.

"Asked for what, exactly?"

"More of a demonstration."

A second later, he found what he was searching for under her seat and produced another strap. This one he banded across the front of her knees, the small spacer in the center pushed between them to hold her legs apart.

"Holy crap!" Her free arm fell off the ledge into the water with a light splash as the bubbly swirls made their way up between her legs to caress the sensitive tissues. Her hips jerked in reaction, and when she tried and failed to close the gap, another intense wave of heat engulfed her.

"Still wondering what the big deal is?" he whispered in her ear, cupping her breast.

It's you, not the bondage, she was tempted to admit, but again wasn't sure. She was sure his calloused palm felt good kneading her breast, his rough thumb brushing her nipple sending more sparks south. "Let's just say it has potential." He tweaked her puckered nub, and she groaned, the small discomfort turning into a pleasant throb before she could take a much-needed breath.

He huffed, a sound between a chuckle and a sigh. "You don't give an inch, do you?"

Poppy slowly lifted her face up to his, stretching to reach his corded neck. "I can, if someone is willing to do the same for me." She nipped his taut skin and leaned back to catch the flame in his eyes before he doused it and shook his head.

"Just this, just tonight, Poppy."

"Then make it worth my while, *Master* Dakota."

He didn't give her time to examine the pang his words wrought, snaking his hand down her abdomen to delve between her thighs. It had been so long since she'd indulged in anything sexual, she wasn't surprised when she splintered apart as soon as he pressed her clit on his way to plunging two fingers deep inside her. She writhed under his pummeling hand, straining against the bonds, her loose hand finding its way to her breast to take over where he left off.

Stars filled the inky blackness behind her closed lids as a hot burst of pleasure swept her from head to toe. She gave no thought to who might see her from inside, to being quiet, or trying to hide her volatile response. She'd waited so long, suffered so much, she deserved to let go with everything in her, to bask and revel in feeling *good*, so damn good for the first time in ages.

Poppy's orgasm was so intense, she lost track of time and her surroundings. By the time she came to groggy awareness, Dakota had her bundled in a towel, held tight against his massive body. Her damp body and the cooler air out of the hot tub finally calmed her racing heart and restored her to full awareness. She looked up, glad for once she couldn't read his face or even guess what he was thinking behind that closed expression, only that he was making no move to take this scene further.

Missing out on the pleasure of wrapping her body around all those rippling muscles caused a tug of disappointment in her abdomen, but regardless, her mission of getting his hands on her was still accomplished. Now she could move on from her interest in this complicated man and concentrate on something or someone new.

Dakota wanted to run, fast and far. He didn't, of course. Once he'd accepted a woman's trust, he didn't betray it, and wouldn't start now. But for the first time since getting into the BDSM lifestyle, the urge to do so gripped him as hard as Poppy's pussy had contracted around his fingers. He never would have pegged her as needy, but once he put his hands on her, and in her, she couldn't hide the flare of desperate longing in her eyes. He could no more resist that unguarded plea than he could walk away without fulfilling his duties.

Her mellow, relaxed state as he hauled her up and wrapped a towel around her slim body spoke volumes about the tension she carried around with her and constantly tried to hide. Never had a woman tempted his pursuit as much as Poppy, and for the life of him, Dakota couldn't figure out why. That self-analysis would have to wait until later though. Right now, the best thing for both of them was to get her dressed and out of here so he could pull himself together and concentrate on his one priority – avenging his mother's death.

CHAPTER FIVE

"Pay attention, girl. It's your move."

Poppy narrowed her eyes at Jerry across the chess table, his irritable voice pulling her head out of the clouds. "I'm thinking." Not about the game, but she didn't say that. She and her boss might have come to an understanding where he tolerated her intolerance toward his less-than-congenial attitude toward everything and everyone, but that didn't mean either of them ventured into revealing personal thoughts. She doubted he would find her obsessive musings about his just-as-recalcitrant neighbor of much interest.

He scowled and shifted his queen. "Not about our game you're not, and that's all I care about."

"You care about Otis, and, from the look of the sheep pens this evening, about your livestock. Good job, by the way." She moved a rook without giving it much thought until he swiped it and she realized her mistake.

"That's what you get for having your head in the clouds," he taunted with a smug look. "What did you do last night that has you so preoccupied?"

The personal question surprised her enough she left her hand hovering above a pawn. Then she smiled, picturing his face if she told him about her hot tub experience, even though it was that memory plaguing her today after she'd awoken craving more from Dakota when she'd expected those hours to have appeased her interest in the man.

"I don't kiss and tell," she replied, widening her grin. "Unless you want to reciprocate."

"I'm not seeing anyone."

She made her move, asking, "Why not? Your wife has been gone for over three years."

Jerry stiffened and glared at her. When she kept her gaze steady, without breaking eye contact, he sighed, his shoulders drooping.

"You don't understand how hard it is to lose someone so special."

"You're right, I don't. But I've been through a rough year of having my life turned upside down from health issues and know how easy it is to get down, to let the depression consume you." Poppy had suffered through her share of despondent days during the worst side effects of the chemo and then the transplant failure.

"How did you get through them?" His eyes slid to his wife's picture and lingered with sadness.

"Honestly, I'm not sure. But I do know if it hadn't been for my parents' unconditional support, I may not have handled it as well. If you'd venture out more, you will see you have just as much support from your and Violet's friends."

"I've got too much to do around here to socialize," he grumbled. "Are you ready to get back to work now that you've had time off?"

"First thing in the morning, Boss." He was well aware she had put in several hours around the ranch despite being officially off, and she still suffered the sore muscles as proof. Of course, her aching body could also be a result of the orgasm that had ripped through her last night and left her reeling today from the swiftness and intensity of her release.

Like she'd been doing all day, Poppy shook off that lingering memory and returned her focus to getting Jerry out more. "You have me to ease your burden around here, so that excuse doesn't cut it anymore. Come up with another one. My friend Lisa called this morning and invited me to a monthly town picnic coming up next weekend. Why don't you start with attending that? She said it's the Rolling Hills' turn to host it, so you only have to go next door."

Jerry ignored her suggestion, saying nothing, so she pushed back and stood, stretching. "I'm beat.

Let's finish later." Reaching down, she petted Otis then headed to the door before he spoke again.

"Poppy, I'll think about it, going to the picnic."

"That's a start," she answered, happy with his concession.

Trekking back to the cabin, Poppy marveled at the beauty of the darkening sunset above the mountains, taking in the deep purple topped with a sliver of amber as the bright-orange ball disappeared behind the tall peaks. Once, she'd thought nothing could compare to watching a day end over an ocean view, but, since coming to Idaho, she had discovered a lot that went beyond her expectations.

Like Dakota's touch.

A pleasant ripple went through her, recalling his plunging fingers rasping her clit with enough friction to set her off within seconds of his penetration. Her groan echoed on the night air, mingling with the constant click of cicadas. How could one man affect her so strongly when others she knew better, even liked more, had taken much longer, or failed altogether to wring such an acute orgasm from her? He'd baffled, frustrated, and excited her from their first chance encounter outside the feedstore and continued to do so weeks later. With any other man, she would have moved on by now, or, at the very least, planned to let the relationship die off.

Instead, the more time Poppy spent with him, the more she craved. Maybe she could whittle it down to an overabundance of stored-up lust, given his freaking awesome body, heart-tripping dark countenance, and the twinge of regret when he hadn't followed up on her orgasm with a bout of fucking. Or it could be as simple as the challenge of his less-than agreeable personality she couldn't resist. But she didn't think so. She couldn't label it, but there was something in his midnight eyes that drew her, the hint of a hardship he struggled with, like she did with her health. Guessing they might share something in common, such as a life-altering ordeal, added to a growing attraction she couldn't deny, and now found herself reluctant to give up on yet.

Her phone rang when she reached the cabin porch, and, seeing her parents' number on the caller ID, she took a seat on the rocking chair then answered.

"Hi there."

"Guess what, Poppy?" her mother gushed.

"You talked Dad into a cruise." Her dad wouldn't go near deep bodies of water, so that would be quite an accomplishment for her mother.

Rose's dry chuckle hit her ear. "No, dear, this is even better. Our investigator thinks he finally has a positive lead on your father."

"I can hear my father in the background and know where he is." Poppy would never think of her sperm donor as her dad.

"Don't be obtuse," Rose admonished. "This is a chance to learn if you have a half sibling or another parent willing to donate. Aren't you excited?"

No, she wasn't. Poppy worried her parents, especially her mother, would take another rejection, either from an unknown relative or her body, even harder than Poppy, and hated to put them through more mental strife, not to mention the strain on their retirement income. Her diagnosis would remain more positive than negative, even without a successful transplant. But if the cancer did return, that would change against her. She understood and sympathized with her parents' fear for her and that possibility but still couldn't stomach them spending so much of their savings on this investigator when the likelihood of some long-lost sibling or father, who never wanted her in the first place, coming to light and then volunteering to help her, a virtual stranger, wasn't good.

"Mom, really, what are the odds? And if

someone is found, what am I supposed to do, show up out of the blue and say, "Hi, I'm the daughter you gave up, or the sister you never heard about, and need your bone marrow. Are you in?"

There was a slight pause before Rose replied, "I'll think of something. In the meantime, how are you doing?"

Her subdued tone and change of subject meant Poppy had gotten to her. Bursting her mother's bubble caused her chest to tighten, but better to face reality now, head-on, instead of getting everyone's hopes up.

"I'm doing good, Mom. You and Dad should plan a trip here soon. It's beautiful, and the people are friendly. I can research tourist attractions in the area, and we can explore them together."

Too bad she couldn't tell her she'd met a nice, interesting guy. That would perk her mother up as it was Rose's dream to see Poppy married with kids. A giggle tickled her throat as she thought of Dakota and labeling him a nice guy. Then she warmed, remembering last night, and couldn't help wishing again for a repeat that went even further. She really wanted to see that man naked.

"I'll mention it to him. I'd better let you go as I'm sure you get up early for work."

"I do, but thanks for calling tonight, and for caring enough to go the extra mile for me, Mom. Love you."

"Always, baby."

Poppy shut off her phone, wondering how she had gotten so lucky. No one could ask for better parents than Rose and Steve, their infertility misfortune a blessing in disguise for her. She hoped she made them proud because she'd never doubted their love for her.

****

Leaning on the corral rail, Dakota eyed the solid-black Morgan mare he'd named Breeze prancing around the enclosure with her head held high, tail up and swinging around her haunches. He couldn't be more pleased with the purchase, her beauty and temperament a good match for Phantom. He planned to introduce the pair in the next few days, since Breeze was acclimating to her new home without any hitches. With luck, she would present him with the start of his breeding program in the next twelve months.

He blew out a breath, frustrated with himself when his mind shifted gears and he pictured Poppy mounted on Breeze, riding alongside him and Phantom, then gravitated to the hot tub scene, regardless of how determined he was to forget it, and her. For two days, he'd been unable to quit thinking about her, her open expressions, soft body, and the tight grip of her slick muscles squeezing his fingers. He'd tried but failed to recall another woman who had come apart under his hands with such swift, high-potency exuberance. When he had held her afterward without counting down until he could let her go and move on, he realized how deeply she had affected him in such a short time.

And that just wouldn't do, not now anyway. He wouldn't even consider delaying his search for Vincent, or his retribution once he found him, for anyone, let alone a woman who didn't suit him. Maybe that wasn't fair, he decided, since there was no denying his constant, growing interest in learning more about her, and why she appeared so frail most of the time. Considering the erection she'd left him sporting after he'd helped her dress and escorted her to her Outlander, something about that too-slender body did it for him. He wasn't a randy teenager who got a boner every time he looked at *Playboy*, and he hadn't turned to someone else to ease his lust.

Whether Poppy suffered from poor health or

was recovering from a bout of illness, she didn't let it keep her down, and he couldn't help but admire her for that. Cynical bastard that he was, he didn't respect or hold too many people in high esteem. Like him, she possessed a drive to see things done right by her own hand, a commendable trait, and worrisome, he imagined, to those who cared about her, given the toll he'd seen it take when she'd come for the straying sheep herself then set about mending fences without waiting for help.

That she could be one of the few he thought highly of threatened his agenda, and he needed to find a way to change course, fast, before he saw her again at Spurs. He knew women — more specifically, he knew sexually submissive women. Not only had Poppy surprised him, and possibly herself, by putting her trust in his hands the other night, but her expressions as she tested the bonds then climaxed while restrained revealed a hidden depth of arousal his control had unleashed. New awakenings such as hers were often mistaken by the submissive for deeper feelings for the Dom. Odds were, she would expect his undivided attention when they saw each other again, maybe even more, and that had to be avoided at all costs as she didn't know enough about him to realize he wasn't looking for a relationship.

Dakota turned at the approach of a vehicle coming up the road, noticing Clayton's Bronco and welcoming the distraction from his thoughts, telling himself as long as he stayed clear of Poppy, he could avoid a sticky situation. Checking the time, he wondered why Clayton wasn't headed into the office. He pulled in front of the stables and got out dressed for court, wearing a jacket and tie with jeans and boots, his Stetson covering only half of his wavy, sandy hair.

"Court or a new case?" Dakota asked him as Clayton joined him at the rail.

"Closing arguments this morning." A shark's satisfied grin split Clayton's face. "I've nailed the thieving bastard cold."

"What did he rob that warrants such glee at seeing him in prison?"

His friend might appear laid-back and easygoing the majority of the time, taking little seriously, but he possessed a ruthless streak when putting criminals behind bars. Even Dakota had winced a few times at the harsh sentences Clayton had won for the poor schmuck unlucky enough to get him as prosecutor.

"Not what, who. An eighty-two-year-old widow living alone. His presence in her bedroom in the middle of the night scared her so bad, she jumped out of bed and ran. Died tripping and falling down the stairs. No way in hell I'm letting him off with a B&E sentence."

Dakota didn't need to see the ice in Clayton's blue eyes as his tone was coated with it. In this case, he agreed with Clayton's anger.

"Okay, he deserves your wrath. What brings you here?"

Leaning a shoulder against the fence, Clayton faced him with arms crossed. "After you left Saturday night, Shawn and I set up a meeting for tonight at Spurs to go over club business and plan a bachelor party there for the McCullough brothers. Ben and Simon are in on the plans. You in?"

He nodded. "I can do that. I suppose Shawn is headed for the same downfall as the McCulloughs."

The three McCullough brothers lived in Snake River Valley, a four-hour drive from Mountain Bend, but two of them, Gavin and Cody, had lived in Boise for a spell and joined Spurs years ago. Whenever they made the drive here to attend auctions or see to other ranch business, they took time to spend an evening at the club. Their recent engagements had come one after the other, not surprising given how close the siblings were, and how fast they'd fallen for their significant others. As attractive as Dakota had found the McCullough's fiancées', he didn't envy the end to their bachelorhood.

Humor shone in Clayton's eyes. "Given the way Shawn doesn't let Lisa out of his sight for long, it wouldn't surprise me. I'm still amazed she remembered us and has kept in touch with Father Joe. All these years, and he never said a word, not even at first, when Shawn kept asking about her."

"He told Shawn he thought it was best for her to move on."

Dakota had no trouble remembering Lisa as a scared nine-year-old, clinging to Shawn when he had carried her out of the Atkins' foster home where they'd all met, or his guilt for not wanting to drag her along with them before he learned of Doyle's visit to the little girl's room. He was happy for the couple now, so that would have to suffice for amends for that lapse in judgement.

"At the time, that was likely the right move. I'd better get going." Clayton took one step then turned with one of his good-humored, lecherous grins. "What's the scoop on this Poppy? Is she a new interest for you, or can I pounce?"

Dakota went rigid, his muscles tightening as he thought of Poppy writhing against Clayton. Because that quick reaction didn't play into his plans to remain free of entanglements, he put a lid on it and forced an expression of indifference.

What came out of his mouth wasn't at all what he'd intended to say. "She expressed an interest in ménage. I'll tag you if she's serious."

"Works for me. Maybe next Saturday, after the picnic."

"Shit, why did we volunteer to hold the first one of the year here?" he grumbled, not liking to take so much time off work and hating the idea of standing around making idle talk all afternoon. What a waste of time.

Clayton slapped him on the back, laughing. "Following in Buck's footsteps, like he would have wanted. Besides, Miss Betty asked us to, and I don't recall you telling her no. You know what a social butterfly she is, and she's looking forward to it."

"And that's the only reason I agreed. I may have to skip the club that night, in need of solitude after spending hours with so many people." Especially since the likelihood of Poppy attending the picnic was good, thwarting his plan to keep away from her.

Pivoting, Clayton headed for his vehicle, tossing over his shoulder, "Fine by me. I don't have a problem taking on Poppy alone."

Dakota straightened from the fence and glared at his friend's back. Clayton knew just how to get to him, part of the sufferance of close friendships he'd had to put up with for twenty years. Given his determination to avoid a sticky situation at the club, not knowing what her expectations were, he would table any decisions until after the picnic and he saw how she reacted.

****

Cars, trucks, and SUVs lined both sides of the long drive into the Rolling Hills Ranch by eleven a.m. Saturday. Poppy was a little late getting to the town picnic, having to keep watch on a difficult birth before she could get away. Jerry had proved he really did care about his responsibility toward his animals by assisting the veterinarian without complaint. Even though her boss had tried to convince her to go, she couldn't bring herself to leave the distressed ewe's side as she'd labored to deliver the breech lamb. All three of them sighed in relief when it was over, and both mama and baby survived.

The only thing marring her upbeat mood from the successful delivery was Jerry's refusal to commit to making an appearance at the picnic. Stubborn old fool, she thought as she found a place to park. If he wanted to spend the warm afternoon alone, she wouldn't let it ruin her day.

The only thing putting a damper on her enthusiasm was going the past week without contact with Dakota. She hadn't realized how much he had impacted her life until they went so long without any chance encounters. For the first time, her decision to move on from a guy had failed to transpire with ease and without regret.

Damn it, she missed the big jerk.

More like she missed the fun of screwing with him. Yeah, that had to be it because no guy had ever meant enough to her to think twice about once he was gone. That's what she'd convinced herself of these last few days, knowing he would attend the picnic on his ranch.

Poppy could see the tables laden with food and more lined with benches and chairs and hiked toward them carrying her pan of brownies to contribute. Several games of horseshoes were in progress and, in a small corral, younger children were beaming atop little ponies. The three-legged race looked fun, but no way would she participate and end up the one falling flat on her face. She recognized Jerry's part-time help at the pond, standing with several other college-age kids, fishing poles in one hand, a beer or soft drink in the other.

Jen saw her and waved her over to her table, and Poppy veered that way. She hadn't met Jen's husband yet but assumed the man sitting next to her was him.

"I don't know what I expected but not this many people. Is the whole town here?" she asked as she reached them.

"Nah, only about half, but that's enough. What did you bring?" Jen nodded at the covered pan.

"Brownies. I figure you can't go wrong with anything chocolate. Is there a dessert table?"

Jen pointed. "The one on the end."

"But I'll go ahead and grab one now. I'm Drew, her"—he tugged Jen's hair as he stood— "one and only."

Poppy shook the hand Drew held out, thinking Jen was a lucky woman. Not only was her husband good-looking, but the way his dark-brown eyes softened when he looked at his wife caused her abdominals to clutch with an odd twist of envy. That was a new feeling for her, and she didn't care for it one bit.

"Nice to meet you," she told Drew. "Here, take your pick." She folded back the foil covering and held the pan out to him.

"They're still warm. Girl, you know how to get a man. Too bad I'm taken."

Jen rolled her eyes behind him, and Poppy chuckled until she spotted Dakota when she glanced over Drew's shoulder. He stood on the far side of the tables with Shawn, Lisa, and the man she recognized as the third owner of the ranch, Clayton, but close enough she could see his guarded expression. What did he think, that she would rush over to him and make a fool of herself because he got her off in the hot tub? She might have missed interacting with him this past week but not enough to throw herself at him.

Poppy lifted her hand in a casual wave then turned back to Drew. "Yeah, that is too bad. Hey, Jen, if you ever get tired of this one, let me know."

Jen chuckled. "Will do, Poppy, but don't hold your breath."

She wouldn't, no more than she would expect Dakota to come chasing after her. "Gotcha. Do you mind saving me a seat while I get a plate?"

"Already done." Jen patted the bench next to her.

"Thanks. Be right back."

Walking over to the dessert table, she didn't

glance toward Dakota again. Instead, she eyed the array of mouthwatering sweets, wondering how many she could sample without making herself sick.

"Hi, Poppy."

She looked up to see Hattie, owner of the deli, approaching holding the hands of two toddler boys. "Hi, Hattie. I'm surprised you remember me. I've only made it into the deli once."

"When you're born and raised in a small town, you remember faces. Take my advice and don't start here or you'll never get to the entrees."

"Good advice." Nodding to the boys, she smiled. "They're cute. Twins?"

"Yes, and in the middle of the terrible twos. But they've behaved and eaten their lunch, so here we are. Oh, those look good," she said as Poppy uncovered her pan and set it down.

"About the only thing I make from scratch. I'd better get my lunch before I cave to the temptation to ignore your advice."

"See you around."

Poppy saw more people she recognized as she strolled down the four long tables of casseroles, plates of fried chicken, vegetable bowls, salads, and homemade breads. Everyone greeted her by name, their warm friendliness chasing away the chill of

Dakota's obvious lack of enthusiasm at seeing her again. She was reaching the end of the row with a plate in each hand piled with more food than she could eat in two days when an amused voice interrupted the temptation to add a hunk of monkey bread.

"I'll bet you a kiss behind the barn you can't eat half of that."

Twisting her head to the side, she met the broad chest of Dakota and Shawn's friend, Clayton, before looking upward. One peek under his tan Stetson confirmed he was as panty-melting at this family-oriented gathering as he was tormenting some poor girl tied up at the club.

She returned his wicked grin with one of her own. "Now, that's a bet worth winning, even if it means I'll pay a heavy price for it later."

"Oh, I like you, girl. I'm Clayton Trebek."

Poppy just realized all the male members of Spurs she'd met so far called all females girl. Being so much younger than Jerry, she expected it from him. It was difficult to rein in the urge to mention she was a woman to them, but she managed since she figured it would be fruitless.

"I know. You were pointed out to me at your club. Poppy Flynn," she replied.

He shrugged his wide shoulders. "I know. You were pointed out to me at the club."

Amused, she leaned forward and whispered, "From what I saw at Spurs, you're not the sneak-a-kiss-behind-the-barn type of guy."

He flashed her another roguish grin. "I could be, for the right girl. For a short time anyway."

Poppy laughed, enjoying his flirting and honesty. "I think I like you, too. Trebek? Any relation to the late *Jeopardy* host?"

"No, but you're not the first to ask. Need any help with that?" He nodded to her two plates.

"Thanks, but I can carry them. Nice to meet you, Clayton."

Poppy pivoted but halted and turned her head when he said, "Let me know if I win that bet."

"You'll be the first," she replied, nodding.

To Poppy's pleased surprise, she spotted Jerry sitting at the end of the same table where Jen was waiting for her. Not only had he made an appearance, but he didn't appear cranky—not overly happy but not put out. She wondered if that had anything to do with the older woman she'd noticed with Dakota now taking a seat next to him and striking up a conversation with an animated look of pleasure at seeing him.

"Who is the woman sitting next to Jerry?" she asked Jen and Drew as she sat down with her plates, shifting her eyes toward her boss.

"That's Betty Cooper. She was good friends with his wife, Violet. You should have seen the jaws drop when he arrived." Jen raised her brows as she added, "You were too busy flirting with Clayton."

"He started it." Poppy picked up a fried chicken breast and took a bite, letting the juices drip down her chin to savor the crispy, seasoned flavor. "*Mmmm, good,*" she managed to get out while chewing.

"There's nothing better than homemade." Drew scraped the last of his salad plate clean then gave Jen a quick kiss before getting to his feet. "I'm going to grab a dessert and join the softball game. Catch you later. Poppy, I hope you'll return to Spurs tonight."

She noticed whenever the club was mentioned in public, caution was taken to talk in low-enough tones the conversation didn't reach anyone else. Being such a small community, Poppy doubted there were too many unaware of the place, or what went on there, but understood the members wanting to protect their privacy.

Pleased with Drew's invitation, she said just as quietly, "I haven't thought about it as it's not my thing, but I did enjoy the socializing, and watching."

He leaned forward to whisper, "From what I saw out on the deck, you enjoyed a whole lot more." With a wink, he straightened and walked away.

Poppy's face warmed, not from embarrassment but the lightning bolt of heat that sizzled through her veins at the reminder of her exhibitionism. She looked at Jen. "Huh, I didn't even see you guys there."

"We came late, not long before you left. Don't worry, Drew would never spread it around you were there."

"Oh, I wasn't thinking that, more along the lines of how much of a new turn-on it is to know people were watching."

Jen giggled. "You are so refreshingly honest, Poppy. That'll come in handy if you hook up with Dakota again. He hates subterfuge from women and gets a lot of it at the club."

Poppy couldn't resist scanning the grounds for Dakota's tall presence and found him at the pony ride, his rare, devastating grin softening his dark face as he helped a little girl onto a pretty white mare. Her heart executed a funny flip at the effect of his full-fledged smile and witnessing his obvious fondness and patience for kids.

A potent combination.

"I doubt we'll get together again," she murmured, dragging her eyes away from the too-enticing scene.

Jen swiveled, took a moment to find what caught Poppy's attention then faced her again with a frown. "I'm sorry. One of us should have warned you about him before you visited the club. He's a good Dom, but don't expect more than an hour or two of his undivided attention."

"Don't worry," she returned, flicking a rueful glance his way again. "I haven't fallen for the guy simply because he gave me an orgasm."

At least, she hoped not. She couldn't deny the immediate draw she experienced the first and every time she'd seen or interacted with him, a compulsion to learn more about him, to be with him again that she'd never felt for anyone else. It had been easy to label it lust then reawakened hormones, but it was still there, a week after that glorious climax, and without hearing or seeing him since.

It did not bode well going forward.

"You're sensible. You would be surprised how many aren't. In that case, I hope you'll return to Spurs, even if it's just to socialize and watch. There are others who come for those reasons alone. You won't need another pass."

Poppy recalled tugging on the hot tub restraints, and the extra spark to her already simmering arousal from the resistance. She still didn't believe she was suited to the lifestyle Jen and Lisa enjoyed but couldn't deny there were some elements that attracted her, such as the voyeurism and exhibitionism. And Dakota.

Crap. Maybe she should return, if for no other reason than to try another mild scene with someone else to drive him from her constant thoughts.

"I might just do that. Thanks, Jen."

"Great. Come on. Let's finish eating then join in a three-legged race. With your long legs, we're sure to win."

"You're on." Anything, even falling on her face in a crowd, was worth undertaking if it demanded her full attention so Poppy could stop pining for that irritable jerk.

****

"I have got to see what that is all about," Shawn told Dakota as Lisa took over for him with the pony rides.

Dakota looked toward Shawn's nod, noticing

Miss Betty still sitting with Old Man Sanders, her face flushed, his guarded but relaxed. He would rather not get involved, but any distraction from Poppy was worth a try. He hadn't been prepared for the sucker punch to his gut upon seeing her again or the instant flashback to the hot tub and her wet, pink body undulating in the water as she exploded in climax. Or her soft voice crying out, close to sobbing with relief, or the innocent way she cuddled against him afterward. Or his reluctance to let her go.

Fuck.

"Let's make it quick. I signed up for the softball game."

Shawn's lips twisted. "Not surprised since you can't socialize while out in the field. Lisa, I'll be right back."

"I've got this. Get the scoop and fill me in," she said, closing the gate behind them.

Dakota turned away as Shawn leaned over and gave her a kiss long enough to draw giggles from the little kids waiting to ride. Unfortunately, his eyes landed on Poppy, again. Wasn't it bad enough to have to deal with the kernel of jealousy poking at him when he'd seen her laughing up at Clayton? Did he really have to admit how goofy happy she looked hopping next to Jen with their legs bound together in a burlap sack? When they toppled over, her peal of laughter resonated between them. She rolled over in the grass, her face as beet red as her tousled hair as they struggled to stand only to fall again.

She was having fun without approaching him. Other than the small wave she sent him when she first arrived, she'd shown no interest in him whatsoever – not what he'd expected. He'd been prepared to evade her advance if she headed his way, had his standard lines ready to deliver that would turn her off from pursuing him if she persisted, so sure she would behave like every other woman.

What the hell prompted him to think that?

Dakota wasn't normally so obtuse about a woman, but then, he'd never met one who'd had such a strong impact on him, and it was taking way too long to diminish or get over her effect on him. But he had no choice. She threatened his agenda, and he wouldn't, couldn't allow that to happen.

"If she's snagged your attention outside of Spurs, you're in a world of trouble."

He whipped his head around to glare at Shawn. "No, I'm not. It just means I need to fuck her and get her out of my system."

Shawn shook his head, his gray eyes turning serious as they walked toward Miss Betty.

"Sometimes it's not that easy. And it's not right to label any woman a simple fuck."

Dakota winced at the reprimand in Shawn's voice. "You're right. She's caught me off guard, thrown me for a loop, and I don't know what to do about it or her. I'm not in the market for a relationship. You know that." Since Poppy continued to show no interest in him, he doubted she would return to the club, where her presence posed the biggest threat to his well-laid-out plans, so maybe he was concerned over nothing.

"I also know you can't go through with your plan if you ever do find the man who killed your mother. You would lose more than you gain," Shawn said, the sore subject between them diverting Dakota's thoughts.

"Your and Clayton's friendship?" He didn't need to look at Shawn to know the risk of that.

"More important, your freedom." Before they were within hearing distance to the table where Miss Betty still sat with Jerry, Shawn paused to say, "Sometimes you have to let the past go to see the future."

"That's easy for you to say," he retorted. "The person who shot your dad is paying for what he did, sitting in prison for life after your dad's cop friends hunted him down, intent on avenging his death."

"You're right, in part, he is paying for his crime. But they stuck to the law they were sworn to uphold, and didn't murder him on sight, even though at the time, I wished him dead," he admitted.

Dakota blew out a frustrated breath, noticing Miss Betty's attention. "I'll figure something out. It's a moot point right now anyway, since I've reached another dead end." He walked forward before Shawn could say anything else.

CHAPTER SIX

Dakota entered Spurs later than usual that night, having gotten delayed by the possibility of new leads in finding the right Vincent. By the time he'd set up the extended searches for two more names, it was already close to ten. He'd thought of texting Shawn and Clayton to ask if they needed him then decided he could benefit more from hooking up with one of the subs. Once he realized he hadn't been with anyone since Poppy had first bumped into him with her mouth full of French fries, he'd driven straight here.

He inhaled the scents of leather and sex, a tantalizing combination that never failed to stir his lust when accompanied by the echoes of soft moans or high-pitched cries following on the heels of bare-flesh slaps. Spotting Ben manning the bar, he veered that way, preferring a beer before scouting for a partner.

"We didn't think you were going to make it in tonight," Ben said, sliding a bottled brew over as soon as Dakota took a seat.

"Me, either. I got sidetracked." Dakota took a

long pull then added, "Good attendance tonight. Am I needed anywhere?"

"Busiest we've had in a while, even with the picnic going on past four. Last I saw, Simon is due to spell Clayton with monitoring, and I just stepped behind here to give Shawn time with Lisa."

Ben nodded toward the closest apparatus, and Dakota eyed the pretty blonde strapped face down on a bench, her full, hard-tipped breasts dangling down from her perch on the padded, narrow center. His friend had lucked out when he'd fallen for a girl already educated in BDSM who was as welcoming of his dominant side as she was of his protective, caring feelings.

"Lucky bastard," Ben said, voicing Dakota's exact thought at that moment.

"Some would think so," he stated, not willing to admit aloud that a part of him agreed for the first time. Then his shifting gaze landed on Poppy's bright-red head tilted up at Clayton where they sat conversing on one of the small sofas, her smile hitting him like a sucker punch to the gut.

"It looks like Clayton might get lucky with our newbie."

Ben's observation cut Dakota to the quick, and he swore beneath his breath. Damn it, did his friends who knew him best have to be right? There was something there, between them, something he'd never experienced with another woman. He couldn't deny it anymore and sure as hell couldn't ignore it, no matter how much a part of him still wanted to, still needed to for the sake of getting retribution for his mother.

"Yeah, he just might but not as lucky as her." Downing the last of his beer, he handed the empty bottle to Ben and rose. "I'll be available to help shortly."

As he started toward Clayton and Poppy, Ben's amused reply drifted to him. "Lucky for all three of you."

Yeah, maybe. That remained to be seen after Dakota tested his feelings and Poppy's admitted interest in experiencing two men at the same time before deciding on where to go from here with the annoying, cute, leggy redhead. When she saw him approaching, her laughing gaze turned wary, her bright-blue eyes dimming. But as he halted in front of her, he spotted the same mix of lust and deeper emotion in those expressive eyes as he felt for her.

Keeping his attention focused on Poppy, Dakota addressed his friend. "Clayton, can I talk you into sharing your plans with our neighbor since she's expressed an interest in experimenting with two men?"

Poppy sucked in a deep breath, her pale face turning pink, but she didn't break eye contact with him. Instead, a small smile played around her soft lips as she slowly crossed her long legs, the move hiking up her snug denim skirt to reveal a few light freckles dotting the upper inside of one thigh.

Dakota's mouth watered to check them out up close.

"I'm in if she is. Sweetheart?" Clayton traced a finger up her neck until he reached under her chin. With a nudge, he turned her to face him, and Dakota knew he was studying her expression as she answered.

"As long as I can back out if I change my mind anytime during, then, yes."

"Say red and we stop, without fail," he replied, his voice rough with the surge of heat to his groin her answer produced.

"Here or in private upstairs?" Clayton asked.

Dakota questioned his sanity when he envied his good friend as Clayton drew his finger sideways to slip under her short curls and circle her ear. He worked at getting himself under control and his head in the game while she took her time to think about those options while scanning the room.

"If it's okay, I'd like to stay here, at least for now."

Poppy's quiet voice never wavered, and her brave determination never failed to win his rare admiration, more so when it was obvious she wasn't altogether sure about him or going forward. "Here, for starters, it is then." Keeping her off guard, building sensation, was key to this being a positive experience for any newbie. He waved a hand, instructing, "Scoot over," before flicking Clayton a look he answered with a smirk and nod, his reaction indicating he'd read Dakota correctly in that he wanted the lead in this scene.

The amused glint in Clayton's eyes meant he was having fun at Dakota's expense. He'd known for a while she was trouble, he mused, settling next to her, but never imagined just how much until now. Picking up her hand, he hoped he wasn't making a mistake as he said, "Let's start with something else you lack experience in, and we'll show you a spanking doesn't always mean a painful punishment."

****

Poppy did not need another thing to question

where her brain had gone the moment she set eyes on Dakota coming toward her. She was already struggling with her easy capitulation after vowing to ignore him tonight and didn't welcome the jitters dampening her immediate arousal when he'd snared her in his intent, black gaze. If it weren't for the comforting clasp of his rough hand enveloping hers, she might have jumped up and stalked off right then, risking missing out on her one chance to indulge herself with two men.

But spanking was nowhere on her list of adventurous sexual things that drew her curiosity.

"I told you I'm not into that." She frowned up at him, the close press of both men's hard strength dwarfing her on the compact settee, heating her blood despite the misgivings his remark caused.

"Then you can use the safeword." Without giving her a chance to reply, or even think, Dakota yanked on her hand, tumbling her over his lap.

By the time Poppy caught her breath, her legs were dangling between Dakota's and Clayton's, leaving her braced on her toes, Clayton's denim-covered thigh pressed against her hip, pinning her lower body in place. Large hands pushed up her skirt and lowered her thong, denying her even that thin band between her cheeks for cover. Her butt clenched, and her mouth opened to protest, but before she could utter a word, two simultaneous hand slaps landed on her unsuspecting flesh, startling her into a gasp instead.

The minor, dual stings didn't last, almost immediately easing into a rather pleasant, warm throb. Surprised, not to mention unsettled by the result, she turned around far enough to see Dakota's face and his hand descend again.

"*Oh!*"

The quick succession of three harder spanks bounced her cheeks and forced her breath from her lungs. "Dakota, wait..."

"Master Dakota, the same for Clayton. Last reminder," he said, this time lowering his hand to smooth away the pain while Clayton did the same on her other buttock. "Is that all you can take? Are you saying red already?"

She recognized the challenging tone, the taunting dare behind the words, but the unexpected, titillating pleasure from their softer caresses robbed Poppy of what few cognitive thoughts she had left. Bemused, turned on, and aching, she gave up and accepted the challenge. Burying her face in her folded arms, she dropped her other hand down to grip his calf and wiggled her butt as much as possible, mimicking the girl she'd watched with interest last week.

"I think your girl just gave us her answer."

She recognized Clayton's amused drawl and prepared herself for Dakota's rejection of Clayton labeling her his girl. Instead, he neither denied it nor agreed with it, his reply leaving her hanging.

"Poppy isn't one to shy away from something new, are you, baby?"

"Just get on with it," she mumbled, the way their hands now rested with light pressure on her butt too distracting and arousing to concentrate for long on anything else.

"You've got your work cut out for you with this one, Dakota."

"Tonight, we do."

They paused long enough to put Poppy on edge then...*holy crap, Batman!* She'd braced for more spanking, not their teasing exploration of her entire backside, their hands roaming every inch of her flesh, cupping the plumper underside of each cheek, kneading each buttock with tight squeezes then releasing. Their calloused palms scratched her sensitive skin, spreading tiny prickles ghosting across her butt. Fingers traced between her cheeks, brushed over her back hole, the light touch revealing sensations both new and tantalizing.

Her brain went to mush, and she melted with the unexpected toss into sensory overload.

I'm not in Kansas anymore. Or is that Houston? Idaho?

Before she could make sense of that thought, their hands left her backside, Dakota's gruff voice instructing, "Deep breath, Poppy," her only warning they were done playing. She obeyed without thought, inhaling as they resumed spanking, adding more force and speed to their smacks. Her blood rushed, and she jolted with the sharper pain, each slap stinging a tad more, burning a touch hotter, and she considered, for two seconds, saying red. Then, like a well-orchestrated team, they returned to softer, comforting strokes over her abused flesh, and she sighed in pleasure instead of stopping them. They were either adept at communicating in silence, or they had earned a lot of experience performing this scene together.

She didn't like picturing Dakota with someone else, so she concentrated on enjoying their attention.

Without warning, the swats resumed, building a myriad of sensations between the heated pain and tantalizing but soothing caresses that stunned her into keeping silent. Instead of turning her off, her body made a liar out of her when the throbbing ache spread and her nipples puckered in response, her pussy swelling with an abundance of cream.

Poppy let her mind go with the pleasurable flow, tuned out the low voices reminding her she lay there with her bare butt exposed to others, her muscles relaxing with her acceptance of this new revelation. She wasn't sure what brought her out of her stupor, or how long she lay there quivering under their hands, only that the spanking and stroking had ended with her entire backside pulsing with a pleasant, aching warmth.

Until they turned her over, effortlessly settling her in front of Clayton with her thighs spread over his, and she groaned from the uncomfortable pressure on her butt. Her first reaction was to complain, but, once again, their quick, deft movements kept her quiet. Looking at Dakota as he went to one knee in front of her, she caught the knowing glint in his dark eyes, her heart executing that funny roll from seeing his mouth tilt at one corner in a devastating half smile.

"What?" she croaked, her throat going dry.

"Time to chase away the pain," was all he said as he stripped her thong off.

Lifting her right leg over his shoulder, he ran

his tongue up her inner thigh, stalling any reply. Clayton raised his hands to the thin straps of her silk top and lowered them to her elbows then cupped her bare breasts, rasping her nipples with his thumbs. She should have been mortified from her exposure in front of people, but that never entered into the current equation, her rising lust the only thing adding up in that moment.

"Relax against me, sweetheart. Let us take care of you," Clayton whispered in her ear, his voice seductive as sin.

"Okay," she agreed without hesitation, no thought necessary. She wasn't stupid, at least not about this and where it was now leading.

They both chuckled at her quick agreement, Clayton's laugh reverberating in her ear, drawing shivers, Dakota's against her spread labia, spiraling up inside her, notching up her heat level.

More please.

As if they could read that thought, they got busy together, Clayton tugging her nipples, pulling her breasts up by the elongated tips then releasing them to knead the plump fullness. Poppy bit her lip as Dakota licked up her seam before pulling her labia open to inch inside her pussy and tongue her clit, sending a lightning bolt of hot pleasure throughout her body. She jumped at the instant contraction of her inner muscles, her breasts turning warm, her nipples now throbbing in tune with her aching glutes as he filled her empty sheath with two thick fingers.

Yes!

Slamming her eyes shut against the onslaught battering her senses, she heeded Clayton's urging and rested against him, shifting her hands to his forearms and holding tight. The storm of pleasure they unleashed upon her was unlike anything she'd experienced before. Clayton tugged on her nipples as Dakota did the same with her clit, the mimicking, dual moves setting off identical flashes of heated arousal. She strained against their hold when Dakota swirled his fingers inside her, scissored them to stretch her muscles then pumped in and out, in and out, all the while suckling her pulsing nerve bundle. Frustration clawed at her, straining to press closer, her sweat-dampened body quivering as Clayton circled his rough palms over her tips then rolled them until she groaned.

Poppy's breathing turned ragged, her body no longer her own. Spots danced behind her darkened lids, her arousal swirling faster and faster, her sheath spasming tighter and tighter around Dakota's pummeling fingers and lapping tongue until she arched and shook with the final explosion of ecstasy.

They didn't allow her to stop there. Clayton shifted her upper body sideways, over one arm, bending his head to suck on one nipple while Dakota pulled his slick fingers from her still-convulsing pussy to tunnel them past the tight resistance of her puckered rear entry. She went rigid at the uncomfortable penetration into that untried orifice then begged for more when his strokes along those hidden nerve endings produced a stunning burst of arousal that ignited a second climax.

Her third release rolled through her as soft and pleasantly slow as their fingers and mouths now were on her nipples, breasts, tender folds, and clit. Instead of returning to full awareness with the last dwindling pleasure, she kept adrift as they righted her clothes and shifted her exhausted, limp body onto Dakota's lap. Unable to help herself, she nodded off to the low murmur of their deep, rumbling voices.

Poppy roused by slow degrees a short time later, achy, still drowsy, and comfortable with Dakota's steady, reassuring heartbeat under her ear. As far as sexcapades went, this one would top anyone's list, but, as she snuggled against his rock-hard chest, a familiar, delicious warmth spread through her tired body, rejuvenating her senses. Now, all she wanted was Dakota to herself, to cap off the night with him hauling her sore butt upstairs and locking them both in one of those private rooms where they could go at it like rabbits until neither could walk.

For whatever reason, he now appeared to have a change of heart about her, and she wasn't above capitalizing on it for as long as it lasted. From the thickness and shape of his erection poking her butt, he was on board with her thoughts.

Turning her face up to his, she smiled.

****

"Welcome back." Dakota placed two fingers under Poppy's chin and lifted her face up to get a good look at her eyes. After making sure the vivid blue was no longer glazed and her head was functioning properly, he nodded, satisfied. As much as he'd like to continue alone with her, she still appeared fragile and tired, and his time would have to wait. "Clayton just left, and you need something to drink, preferably water. Up." He patted her thigh and helped her stand.

"I am thirsty," she said as he took her hand.

"That doesn't surprise me, but you continue to do so." He didn't elaborate even though she flicked him an encouraging look.

The truth was, her acceptance and responses to that scene were everything two Doms could want, but it was also the first time he'd grown unsettled during a ménage. Watching his friend touch Poppy hadn't stirred his lust like the other times they'd shared a woman. Not only did he have to give her time to recover, he needed to decide where to go from here because keeping away from her, or telling himself she was an annoying pest, was no longer working.

"There's Lisa. I'll leave you with her while I spell Simon from monitoring. Be sure you down a whole bottle of water," he insisted as they reached the bar.

"I heard you," Shawn called from the other end. "Be right there."

"Thanks." He glanced at Lisa, missing Poppy's look of disappointment as he asked her, "Do you mind keeping Poppy company until she's ready to go?"

"Of course not." Lisa frowned at him, but he had enough trouble figuring out one woman; he wasn't about to trouble himself with another.

"Poppy, come find me when you're ready. I'll walk you out to make sure you're okay to drive."

She waved an airy hand, averting her face as she replied, "I'm fine, Master Dakota. You don't have to bother."

He swore. For some reason, her dismissive attitude and emphasis on his title pissed him off, but he didn't have the time to try to figure her out right now. "It's no trouble. Come get me."

She didn't reply, just took the water as Shawn walked up with it, smiling at him and starting up a conversation with Lisa. Blowing out a frustrated breath, he spun and stalked off, needing to put space between them before he throttled her, or forgot his good intentions and hauled her upstairs. She'd probably like that but would pay a hefty price come morning.

He'd gone into that ménage thinking there was something brewing between them, and he now knew it was stronger than he'd first guessed, at least for him.

"From what I witnessed, your scene with our newbie went well, so why are you scowling?" Observing the room from the back, Simon appeared relaxed leaning against the wall, but Dakota saw the way he kept an eagle-eyed watch on the room.

"She's been driving me nuts since we met." Simon let out a laugh loud enough to draw heads and irk him even more. "What the fuck is so funny?"

Simon's gold loop earring shone as he shook his bald head, his grin never slipping despite Dakota's irritation. "Think about it, Dakota. I'm assuming you're here to relieve me, and, after watching you and Clayton with the lovely redhead, I'm more than ready to play."

"First, tell me all is going smoothly. I'm not in the mood for a confrontation with anyone."

"No worries there. Later."

Dakota took Simon's place and scanned the crowd, refusing to let Poppy's mood interfere with his job. He would question her again when she'd had time to mellow, and he walked her out. Until then, let her stew since she'd insisted she was fine. But when he returned to the bar after coming inside from checking the deck and saw Lisa sitting with Kathie, and Poppy nowhere in sight, he cursed.

"Where is she?" he barked, causing two girls seated a few stools down to jump up and leave. Watching them take off, he realized he'd never scared Poppy away, which turned his irritation with her to concern. "Is she all right?"

"She was fine," Lisa said, resting her small hand on his rigid arm. "Just tired and ready to go. I tried to get her to wait, or to find you and tell you, but she insisted on not bothering you."

"I'm free, Master Dakota." Kathie batted her eyelashes with exaggerated flirtatiousness.

She was attractive, soft in all the right places, and fun to play with, but he didn't want Kathie. Yeah, he had some more serious thinking to do before he saw Poppy again. In the meantime, he'd give her tonight and tomorrow since he promised Ben he would track that wounded bear, which could take most of the day.

"Another time, Kathie."

Dakota nodded and pivoted to return to monitoring, missing Lisa's murmured, "Oh, he really has it bad," and the small, knowing smile that accompanied her comment.

****

Dismounting, Dakota eyed the fresh tracks along the trail, the bright drops of blood easy to detect against the twigs and ground cover of the wooded path. The forest became less dense the closer they'd gotten to the summit of this hill, and they could hear the rev of ATVs not far off. He didn't like how new these current tracks were, considering the terrain in this area of rolling hills was a popular draw for hiking, mountain biking, and trail running. There were too many people and opportunities for a pain-crazed grizzly to attack again.

"He's definitely injured, and, from the amount of blood loss we've found this afternoon, it's bad," he told Ben, who remained mounted.

"Fucking pisses me off, but nothing to be done now except get to him before he comes across anyone else. Ready?"

"Let's move."

He swung up into the saddle and nudged Phantom to follow Ben as they set out again. The bear had wandered in and out of the trees, on and off the trail, his pattern making no sense. That told Dakota infection might have spread to the animal's brain, which heightened the urgency of the hunt. They'd been at it since midmorning, taking only one break to down a packed lunch, and had a good hour's ride back to the ranch ahead of them unless they camped out.

Dakota didn't relish that idea. Not only would they have to take turns sleeping to keep watch, but he was hoping to return home in time to call Poppy before she went to bed. By the time he'd touched base with the weekend hands on their chores and started another search on what his best lead might be yet in finding Vincent, Ben had arrived, chomping at the bit to start their tracking.

They rode in silence for another fifteen minutes, the tracks leading them east then a slow turn south, back down the rugged rise and closer to the possibility of outdoor activities. A tortured growl rent the air, bringing them to a halt, sending a frisson of alarm through Dakota. The horses shifted in agitation at how close the bear's cry echoed, and he hoped this meant they were near the end of their search.

"To the left?" Ben asked.

"That's my guess."

They lost the trail, staying on the path, and veered into the rougher terrain of the woods to pick it up again. Talking wasn't necessary; the bear's continued angry snarling and blood splatter was enough to lead them in the right direction. They came upon him unexpectedly, entering a copse that would have been a good place to pitch a tent as it was one of the fire lookouts scattered around the Boise Mountains. Luckily, the massive grizzly was alone, his furious frustration aimed at a treed raccoon shaking in terror on a limb out of his reach. From his blood-soaked side and front right leg, the bear was in too much pain to climb after the critter.

"He's barely hanging on," Ben said quietly, pity and anger in his resigned voice.

"Meaning, we don't have a choice." Which pissed Dakota off to no end. What a tragic demise for such a magnificent animal.

He and Ben reached for their rifles at the same time, pulling them from the scabbards, taking aim and firing when the wounded, enraged grizzly saw them and charged. The woods echoed with their rapid gunfire and the bear's last roars before a hushed, eerie silence fell with his large body. They waited a few moments, making sure he didn't move again, then dismounted, keeping their rifles cocked and ready as they approached the downed animal.

"What a fucking shame." Ben crouched and examined the dead grizzly's wound, swearing under his breath as he stood again. "A skilled hunter would never hit any animal in the joint like that, knowing the pain they'd inflict if a kill shot missed."

"And even those new to the sport should know better than to leave it to suffer, and to report a wounded, possibly dangerous animal. It's doubtful you'll find him."

Ben pushed his hat up and gave Dakota a direct look, his green eyes serious as he said, "You could apply some of that tenacious effort you've put into your personal search and help me."

Dakota stiffened then relaxed, refusing to rise to the bait. He was aware others knew of his search for Wiyaka's killer, but only Shawn and Clayton were privy to his intentions once he found the man. "I hope you're not comparing my mother's deliberate murder to the possibility of a bear's deliberate injury," he returned coolly.

"No, so don't get bent out of shape. I'm saying your tracking skills aren't limited to finding outdoor clues, if you want to do some searches of hunters in the area."

He swung his rifle onto his shoulder with another glance at the bear, noting it had taken six bullets to end his misery. "Yeah, I can check against hunting licenses and camping permits, to start. For now, let's get out of here."

Ben agreed with a nod. "Not much else to do for the poor guy except send someone to haul down the carcass for a necropsy. Retrieving the bullet might help in our search."

Sunset was a thin, amber glow on the western horizon as Dakota and Ben parted upon reaching Rolling Hills property again, and the spot where Ben had left his truck and horse trailer. He waited until Ben's taillights disappeared down the road before turning Phantom toward home, his thoughts once again straying toward Poppy. Something about the bear's pain reminded him of her, a look in the animal's eyes, or a note in his last huffs that made him think of her. Which was odd, considering he'd never seen her in pain.

He supposed the look he'd caught on her face as he'd led her toward Lisa last night could be labeled hurt, but since she was the most confusing woman he'd ever met, what the hell did he know? From the way she'd embraced every touch of his and Clayton's hands and mouths, and the number of orgasms they had driven her to, he couldn't fathom what her expression meant.

As if thinking about her had conjured her up, her soft, somewhat slurred voice filtered through the trees separating their properties. Reaching the fencing he'd repaired, he saw her perched on the rail, tilting a liquor bottle to her mouth.

"Poppy, what the hell are you doing out here?"

CHAPTER SEVEN

The ground shook and almost toppled Poppy off the fence. Once she regained her balance, she looked up, and her heart squeezed as she imagined the large shapes of Dakota and his horse out in the pasture, just like the first time she'd seen them. They looked so real, she could blame her near fall on Phantom's fast hoofing impacting the earth and Dakota for interrupting her drunken musings. She wasn't happy about the distraction. She'd grabbed the bottle of whiskey and gone for a walk in hope of ridding her thoughts of him and the lingering hurt from his second rejection. When her fuzzy brain put her in jeopardy of getting lost, she'd trekked to the place her infatuation had begun, settled on the rail, and attempted to purge her mind of the irritating, sexy, rude, sexy, obnoxious, sexy...oh hell, there went her scrambling musings again.

She took another long pull of the fiery alcohol then shook her head and blinked her eyes as the blurry image of horse and rider stopped in front of her. Gripping the wood rail with her free hand, she raised the bottle, saluting the apparition.

"And there he is, my midnight rider, returning to the scene of the crime. Go 'way. You...you're not invited to my pity party."

"Poppy, what are you doing out here? It's almost dark."

"Oh damn, even when your voice is a pigment of my 'magination, my toes still curl. Knock it off."

"I'm not a figment of your imagination. Why are you having a pity party?"

"'Cause of you, you big lug. Now, shoo! You. Are. Not. Here. Just a pigment...well, something." As long as he went away, she decided it didn't matter.

"Figment, and I'm..."

"Look, buddy, I have three degrees and two... two...well, two other pieces of paper that prove I'm not stupid, so quit correctin' me," she snapped.

The image tilted his head in that sexy manner he had, and she went warm imagining those dark eyes shielded by his Stetson focused on her, just her.

There was enough remaining light to make out his slow, devastating grin, the one that turned her all mushy inside. Then he had to go and ruin it by opening his mouth.

"You're cute when you're drunk."

She bristled, and the warm mushiness disappeared. "Cute? Cute!" *Did I just screech like a banshee? Yep, I think I did.* "I'll have you know, Mr. Hotshot, I can get anybody..." His horse shifted and they grew blurry again, causing her to lose her balance and train of thought as she tightened her hold on the fence and the bottle. *Can't drop that.*

"Yes, cute. Have me know what?"

"Huh?" *Where was I? Oh yeah.* "I'll have you know I wasn't a bad catch before the big C got hold of me." She waved the bottle in front of her. "Just because I have a few more pounds to put back on, and I still get tired easily..." His frown confused her, derailing her thoughts.

He inched nearer, until that big, beautiful stallion was close enough she could smell his earthy scent and feel his warm breath on her arm. *Oh, dear, maybe not my imagination. Damn, I hate it when he's right.*

"Big C? Cancer?"

It was Poppy's turn to frown. Why was he still here, and, more important, why was she spilling personal beans after he'd rejected her twice. She took another swig then blinked her blurry eyes, fairly sure he was the real McCoy, or cowboy, or Dom, or royal pain in the ass who had her tied up in knots from day one.

"Go away. You're the reason for my pity party

and weren't invited." That line sounded familiar, maybe because he wasn't listening.

"You're on my side of the fence. I don't need an invitation. What did I do last night that upset you? You enjoyed everything Clayton and I did."

"You're right." Poppy hiccupped, recalling his every touch and his rejection. "But then you dumped me, again, when I wanted..." She clamped her mouth shut and glared at him.

Dakota regarded her in silence for several unnerving moments before he replied in a surprised tone, "You think I didn't want you? Baby, nothing could be further from the truth."

She started to shake her head, grew dizzy, and stopped. "You're just saying that now 'cause you feel sorry for me." Lifting the dwindling bottle, she drank again, the thought of him pitying her souring her stomach. She could accept anything but that.

He shrugged those massive shoulders, saying, "I like to think I have empathy for anyone who goes through a rough ordeal. But, again, you're wrong. I wanted you after the hot tub, and last night, but both times you were too wiped out to take things further, and part of a Dom's job is to take care of his partner's needs, all of them. Since you're new at it, you didn't know that."

No, she hadn't, but when she remembered seeing Lisa and Shawn together, she realized she should have. The warm mushiness returned.

"Aww, you're so sweet. You're not the badass everyone thinks you are."

"Yes, I am. Ask any other girl at Spurs. Most run from me in fear."

She snorted. "Wimps."

"Yes, but you're not, are you, baby? You've stood up to me from the beginning."

No, no, no. This will not do. I refuse to give in to that deep voice or my betraying body. "Since I can't make you go away, I will." She tried swiveling around, but the ground spun in circles below her, and she lost her balance.

"*Whoa!*" she cried out as his thick arm scooped her off her perch and onto his lap. Finding herself right back where she wanted to be, yet didn't want to be, robbed her of what little sense she had left. Before she opened her mouth on what she wanted to say, she blurted, "Where's the bottle?"

"On the ground, where it's staying until I return tomorrow to pick it up," he answered, tugging the reins to turn Phantom.

Crap. I'm only human. Between the slow rocking against Dakota's hard, warm body with the horse's movement, and his heartbeat under her ear, his rumbling voice above her, she lost the battle and caved to her baser needs.

Gripping his forearm, Poppy turned her face up to his, barely able to make out his strong jaw in the dark, and pled, "Kiss me, Dakota. Just like you did the first time at Spurs, when I forgot everything and didn't have to think. Pretty please?"

He tightened his arm, hugging her as he replied, "Not while you're inebriated, Poppy."

God! How could she get angry when he was looking out for her? How freaking frustrating! "You are such a party pooper." She sighed. "I don't know why I like you so much."

"If it's any comfort, you're not alone there. I can't fathom why I like you so much, either. You're coming home with me, Poppy, and we'll work this out, whatever it is between us, in the morning."

"Okay."

For the second time in twenty-four hours, Poppy fell asleep on Dakota's lap, trusting him to take care of her.

****

Dakota arrived back at the stables still

shaken from Poppy's disclosure about suffering from cancer. He'd gone cold hearing that, his first thought, *not my Poppy*, which had also given him a jolt. His stubborn blindness concerning her was unacceptable once he'd crossed the line at Spurs from an acquaintance to her first Dom, even though she would never admit she possessed a small thread of sexual submissiveness. He'd always taken his responsibility in accepting a woman's submissive trust seriously, and the fact he'd let Poppy down left him raw with guilt.

Looking down at her tousled red head resting with such trust against him, he recalled her brazen, cheeky forwardness and would have sworn the woman didn't have one insecure bone in her slender body before tonight. But after hearing the catch in her voice, and the hurt when she mentioned him turning away from her, he realized he was wrong. He'd bet his left nut that kernel of self-doubt over her desirability was a result of her recent physical ordeal.

Poppy's underweight appearance and seemingly low energy now made sense, and, as he reined in Phantom and dismounted with her in his arms, the urge to feed her gripped him. Shaking his head at this turnabout of his feelings toward her, he lowered her legs and held her as she stirred.

"Wake up a minute, Poppy. I need to see to Phantom before we go in."

In the dim glow of the stable's outdoor lighting, he watched her blink her eyes open and look around with her slim brows dipped in confusion. Reaching out to his horse, she gave his neck an absent pat.

"Nice pony," she mumbled.

Dakota wasn't sure his sixteen-hand, fifteen-hundred-pound stallion would care for the term pony, but Phantom was a good sport. "Yes, he is. Sit down a minute while I get someone to bed him down."

She perked up at that, her lips kicking up in one of those flirty grins as he nudged her onto the bench outside the stable. "Then are you going to bed me down?"

"Yes, but not in the way you think."

At least, not yet, he thought, turning away from her puzzled frown. That would happen when she was sober, and there was no doubt in her mind about his actions or intentions. Rectifying his mistake in dealing with her didn't include leading her on. He cared about her, more than he had any other woman, but that acknowledgment didn't mean giving up his twenty-year quest to avenge his mother's death.

Entering the stable, he spotted Rick and waved him over.

"Hey, Boss. Are you just getting back?"

"Yes, and yes, we finally found him. Ben was right, he'd been severely injured, but he's not suffering anymore. Can you bed Phantom down for me? I have a guest I need to take care of."

Curiosity shone on his face as Rick nodded. "Sure." Then they stepped outside where Poppy waited. "Ah, the cute redhead," he commented with a hint of amusement.

"Yes, the cute redhead. Thanks."

Dakota snatched Poppy's hand and led her up to the house, ushering her inside and closing the door without looking at Rick again. She must have gotten a second wind because she practically skipped alongside him as he drew her upstairs and into his bedroom, but, having been inebriated before, he knew her burst of energy wouldn't last.

She stumbled to a stop behind him, bumping into his back when she saw his bed. "Oh, wow, that is one big bed."

"I'm one big guy."

Wrapping her arms around him from behind, she giggled. "Yeah, I noticed that right away. Hard to miss." She hiccupped then added, "So was your cranky attitude."

"And yet you didn't run away." He pulled her in front of him and divested her of her T-shirt and bra.

"I thrive on challenge. Touch me, Dakota."

"No, not tonight, and don't give me that betrayed look. In the morning, we'll talk first then I'll fuck you." He yanked her jeans down, along with her panties. "Step out."

Grabbing his shoulders, she did as instructed, muttering, "And you call me st...stubborn. *Whoa,* slow the presses, would ya?"

Scooping her swaying body up in his arms, he said, "They'll slow once you're lying down and sleep."

"I'm naked and horny, and you think I...I'll sl... eep?" She yawned as he laid her on the bed and flung the covers over her.

"I know you will."

Dakota watched her snuggle down and lose the battle to keep her eyes open. Her soft snores were the only sounds in the room as he walked out.

****

Poppy awoke to a raging headache, sunlight blinding her as she struggled to get her eyes open, and a roiling stomach. *Why did I drink so much?*

She hadn't gotten that drunk since her early twenties when she was in a college sorority. While undergoing chemo, the last thing she'd needed was additional bouts of nausea. Rolling over, she shivered as the soft sheets brushed her bare skin, and she remembered Dakota's big, warm body wrapped around her most of the night.

She scanned the bedroom, made note of the large dresser, a comfortable-looking stuffed chair in the corner, and the window that offered a view of a well-tended green lawn and, beyond, pastures dotted with cattle. Her gaze landed on the end table, and the glass of orange juice, two aspirin, note, and picture.

There was no mistaking Dakota as the boy of ten or twelve next to the beautiful woman with her arm wrapped around him, the family resemblance unmistakable. Poppy assumed the woman was his mother, and she wondered where she lived now and why he'd never mentioned her. Then again, before last night, neither had shared personal information. Most men would have taken her home last night and been done with her after hearing the word cancer, but the fact he'd brought her here and held her all night gave her a small kernel of hope they were entering a new phase of their relationship. One that included lots of time under, over, and clinging to that awesome body.

Picking up the note, she read: Help yourself to the shower then come find me in the kitchen.

"Still a man of few words," she mumbled, reaching for the juice and downing the aspirin.

Running through what she could remember in her head, Poppy only regretted feeling poorly this morning. She hadn't hidden her interest in Dakota since they'd met, so she wasn't mortified by what she recalled telling him. As long as she hadn't mistaken his caring for pity, she could face him this morning with her head high. If he showed any sign of feeling sorry for her, she'd give him a piece of her mind then leave, even if that were the last thing she wanted to do.

First, a long, hot shower sounded divine. One of Dakota's black T-shirts lay at the foot of the bed, and, with something close to tenderness joining the heated rush of arousal traveling through her veins, she picked it up and padded into the adjoining bathroom.

A charming clawfoot tub took up a corner, but the blue-and-white subway-tiled shower big enough to hold four appealed more right now. Indulging herself, she turned on all four showerheads and took her time absorbing the steam into her pores. By the time she emerged, her skin red from the hot water, her headache gone, and her stomach now rumbling with hunger, she was as ready as she'd ever be to face the lion in his den and see where she stood with him today.

All Poppy had to do to find the kitchen was follow the enticing coffee and bacon aromas that hit her as soon as she left the bedroom. At the bottom of the stairs, she glanced into a small, charming sitting room then veered right, walking into a large living, dining, and kitchen area where it was obvious walls had been removed to open up the space.

And then Dakota's broad, tanned back snagged her gaze, and she forgot all about his appealing farmhouse. Pausing by the stone fireplace, she took a moment to enjoy watching him at the stove, admiring his nice ass in snug denim and the way his wide shoulders tapered to slim hips. His straight black hair was pulled back in his usual style, and, if she wasn't mistaken, he was humming as he risked getting splattered with bacon grease.

"Do you feel up to eating?" Dakota turned and pinned her in place with his focused, dark-eyed stare before nodding and saying, "You look better. Come on over and sit down." He waved his two-pronged fork toward a small table in the bay window alcove.

"I'm surprised I want to eat, but who can resist bacon and coffee?" A thrill shot through her when he didn't try to hide his interest in her bare legs below his oversized shirt as she strolled toward the table.

"I never could when I indulged, which I haven't done to the extreme you did for over a decade." Scooping eggs and bacon onto two plates, he carried them over. "We'll discuss that while we eat. Get started while I pour your coffee. How do you like it?"

"Lots of cream and sugar," she replied, looking up at him as he set the plates down.

"Good, you can use the calories, and don't get your feelings out of whack again. That's a simple observation you have already acknowledged."

She lifted a brow, her lips ticking up in amusement. "Out of whack?" He scowled, and she fought back a giggle. That was more like him.

"You know what I mean. But I'll admit I was at fault for your previous wrong presumptions about my actions that led to your pity party."

He frustrated her by leaving it at that instead of explaining when he pivoted and strode to the coffee pot near the stove. She let it go for now in favor of scooping up some eggs. "Thank you," she said as he set a steaming mug in front of her, "for everything, last night and this morning."

"You're welcome." Taking a seat, he took several bites before surprising her by asking bluntly, "What kind of cancer do you have?"

"Well, that's straight to the point."

Looking up, he gave her a direct stare. "You opened up the subject, now finish. I'm assuming you're not in treatment now."

"No, I'm doing good, in remission. Hodgkin's lymphoma is curable, more so with a successful bone-marrow transplant." She bit into a piece of crispy bacon, thinking that was enough.

Apparently, not for him.

"And did you have one, or are you on a list?" he asked while chewing.

Poppy sipped her coffee, regarding him over the rim before answering. His interest seemed genuine, not nosy, and she supposed if she wanted more from him for the time being, she shouldn't resent his probing.

"One failed transplant." She shrugged, as if it didn't matter. "A familial donor would be best, but I'm adopted, and my birth mother, the bitch, still wants nothing to do with me, which is fine by me. Anything else you want to know?"

He chewed, regarding her with another intense

look that poked at her patience before replying, "I agree, she's a bitch. No chance of someone on your father's side offering?"

She sighed, seeing no way out of his probing except full disclosure. "My *real* parents are trying to find him despite my disagreement on the subject. I'm fine now, my prognosis is still good without tracking down some stranger with my DNA, but I can't convince them of that."

"They love you."

She smiled. "Yeah, they do. I'm lucky. I saw your photo next to the bed. Where's your mother?" She wasn't prepared for the anger tightening his face or the emotion swirling in his eyes. He was about to deny her that information, but she stopped him before he said anything. "Turnabout is fair if you want any more to do with me after this morning. I opened up to you, and I'm not drunk now."

Dakota set his fork down and took a deep breath, as if bracing himself against her reaction. "You're right. My mother's dead, murdered, and I won't rest until I find the man responsible."

His hard, implacable tone sent a shiver down her spine, but his words shocked her into sympathy. "Oh shit, Dakota, I'm sorry." That was the last thing Poppy expected him to say. "Do the cops have any leads?"

A tic jumped in his granite jaw, she imagined from clenching his back teeth. "They quit looking years ago, then I took over." With an abruptness that startled her, he pushed to his feet and gathered up their empty plates, carrying them over to the sink before tripping her pulse with a look of undisguised pure, carnal lust.

Poppy went hot all over and forgot about everything except how much she wanted him, craved him unlike any other man she'd been involved with. He approached the table with a slow, predatory stealth that turned her mouth dry and her pussy damp.

"What are you doing, Dakota?" she asked as he grasped her upper arms and pulled her up.

"Making sure this time you don't leave with a misconception." Shoving the chair out of the way with his bare foot, he lifted her onto the table.

Given the state of her panties, her first concern was over the embarrassing risk of leaving evidence of her arousal on the table. Then he whisked the T-shirt over her head, and her only spare thought was for protection. He cupped her breasts, and her breathing hitched, but she managed to ask, "Do you have a condom?"

"I wouldn't have started this if I didn't."

Bracing her hands behind her, Poppy leaned back with a teasing tilt of her pelvis. "Then, what are you waiting for?"

With what she could only describe as a low growl, Dakota lifted one hand to fist a wad of her short curls to anchor her head in place. Lowering his face, he pinched her nipple hard enough to draw a gasp.

"I call the shots, baby. Remember that."

Before she could gather her wits to form a reply, he covered her mouth and kissed her with ruthless intensity that spread tingles down to her toes, just like his first kiss at Spurs. By the time he let her up for air, her panties were on the floor, and his hand had left her breast to wrap around his thick erection.

"You won't fit," she stated without thinking, unable to pull her eyes away from his smooth mushroom cap and already seeping slit.

"Yes, I will." Releasing his cock, he kept hold of her hair with his other hand as he spread her legs by moving in between them. "Lie back."

Poppy shook her head. "No way. I want to watch."

He muttered something she couldn't make out then worked two fingers inside her sheath, tunneling slow but steady until she had no choice but to go with the flow of warm pleasure he was so good at building into a fiery inferno. The three-paned bay window invited the morning sun to splash across her torso, the toasty effect as arousing as Dakota's hot potent gaze and pumping hand igniting a fire deep inside her inner core. Her pussy clenched around his thrusting fingers, her breathing growing shallow as he milked her clit, ratcheting her up another notch.

"Dakota." His name spilled from her lips in a tortured whispered plea, her muscles quivering from straining against his hand.

Dipping his head again, Dakota drew on one nipple, the strong suction of his lips unleashing waves of pleasure to add to the pulsations squeezing his marauding fingers. Arching her neck, Poppy closed her eyes and basked in the spiraling myriad of bursting sensations, loving his equal attention to both nipples as he slid his mouth to close around the opposite nub.

Desperate now for the final push, she lifted her head and opened her eyes, resorting to demanding instead of begging. "Damn it, Dakota, I can't get any more ready."

Hearing the strain in Poppy's voice and feeling

it in her damp, gripping muscles, Dakota released her nipple and her hair and straightened. His eyes on hers, he pulled from the tight resistance of her slick pussy, grabbed her right hip, and turned her pelvis sideways enough to deliver a hard smack on her ass. She glared at him but clamped her lips together as her nipples puckered into even harder pinpoints.

"We need to work on you making demands during sex," he stated, reaching for the condom he'd laid on the table earlier. "I'll know and will say when you're ready. Any other phase of our relationship, I'll respect your voice and independence as long as you give me the same whenever I put my hands on you."

"I'm not used to..." Her blue eyes wandered down to watch him sheath his cock, and she seemed to lose her train of thought until she muttered, "Oh hell, whatever."

"That'll do for an answer, for now."

Dakota cupped her legs under the knees and lifted them over his arms, pulling her hips to the very edge of the table before sliding under her to clasp her buttocks. He smiled, watching those expressive eyes widen then glaze over as he dragged his cock up between her glistening folds, a visible shudder going through her body.

She released her breath with a husky, "*Oh.*"

Unable to keep toying with her without risking ending this too soon, he pushed inside her pussy, stopping when those soft folds enveloped his cockhead. "Take a deep breath."

Poppy nodded, watching with unabashed rapture as he circled his way deeper inside her pussy, working through the tight muscles, aided by the abundance of cream his fingers had produced. She mewled, and he stopped, looking up at her face.

"No, don't you dare stop. I'm fine, more than fine."

"Then, brace yourself." Taking her at her word, he pushed farther, going until she'd accepted half his length. Now, there was no going slow. Pulling back but not completely out, he set up a slow, steady rhythm that stole both their breaths. The hot friction of her responsive body pulled him in and fought his withdrawal, her gasping litany of *yes, more*, egged him into picking up speed. As her contractions increased, threatening to cut off his circulation, she dropped down to her elbows and strained against his hold, begging and cursing at the same time.

Satisfied, Dakota gave in to his own raging lust and let go, spewing into the condom with numbing lightning bolts of pleasure that threatened his sanity.

"Hold on, and I'll help you," he said when the fog cleared from his mind and he withdrew from Poppy's still quivering pussy.

He should have known she wouldn't let a simple thing like a mind-blowing orgasm stop her from letting him know the sex was over and his control ended. She scooted off the table as soon as he stepped back, bending to retrieve her panties and treating him to a nice view of her ass. Seeing the pink remnant of his swat, he couldn't resist trailing his fingers over it as she straightened.

"You'll think of me today," he said, liking that idea maybe a bit too much.

Poppy turned, slipped her panties on and pulled them up, replying, "I would have without that to remind me." Going on her toes, she surprised him by whispering, "Thank you, *Master* Dakota," before pressing her lips softly against his.

Before he could take over, she pulled away with a laugh and danced out of reach, her breasts swaying as she snatched his T-shirt off the chair. Donning it, she emerged from the neck with a regretful sigh. "I have to get going, even if I don't punch a time clock."

"You're welcome. Go get dressed. I'll use the hall bath then drive you over."

Her eyes gleamed as she glanced at the full condom. "I can help with that chore."

"Not unless you want to be even later." Taking her shoulders, he spun her toward the hall and gave her a small push, smacking her butt as she headed that way.

With a grunt laugh, she skipped ahead, tossing over her shoulder, "We're going to have to discuss this spanking fetish of yours."

"Nothing to discuss," he shot back, a pleasant warm sensation rolling through him as he followed then veered into the front bathroom.

She didn't take long, and they met in the hallway a few minutes later. "I have to grab a shirt and my boots."

"I'll wait out front."

Dakota finished dressing quickly, hoping her hurry to leave was due to work obligations. For the first time, he wasn't anxious to part company with a woman now the sex was over. How she'd dug under his skin when he'd done everything to avoid that escaped him, but, for now, he would accept he enjoyed her company enough to keep her around for a while.

The sounds of a busy, working ranch greeted him as always when he stepped onto his porch. He never tired of hearing cattle lowing in the distance, the occasional horse whinny, hooves clomping around the corrals, his hired hands joking with one another. But this morning, he paid less attention to the familiar and zeroed in on the uncommon sight of a woman he was involved with standing at one of the corrals, smiling at Chuck. Even rarer was seeing his foreman returning her smile, as Chuck's gruff personality matched Dakota's.

Breeze came prancing over as he approached the pair, and Poppy turned that mega-watt grin on him. "She's gorgeous, Dakota. And I love her name."

He sent Chuck an inquiring glance, which he returned with a sheepish shrug then tipped his hat to Poppy and walked away. Bemused, Dakota moved next to Poppy at the rail.

"Thanks. I'm pleased with her, and Phantom is enamored, which is good."

"Why?"

"I'm planning on breeding them. Morgans are a versatile breed and should bring in a nice profit." He stroked the mare's nose then down her neck the way she liked.

Poppy joined him, sifting her delicate fingers through Breeze's silky mane. "I'd become too attached and keep all of them."

"I didn't know you were a horse lover."

Pulling her hand back, she turned. "There's a lot we don't know about each other. I'm ready if you are."

Taking her hand, he shortened his steps to match hers as he led her to his Jeep. "We can work on that. How about a ride, you on Breeze, sometime this week?"

Opening the door, he watched a dumbfounded expression cross her face. It seemed she wasn't expecting his change of attitude, either.

"I'd like that, but I'm surprised you would."

"Yeah, well, a lot about you has surprised me, too. Get in."

CHAPTER EIGHT

Houston

❝I swear, David, I don't have a clue. Maybe it's one of your competitors trying to dig up dirt to use against you."

Constance paced the sunroom with her phone to her ear, her husband's call catching her off guard. To hear her assumption the Flynns had dropped their pursuit of a family donor for their daughter had been mistaken angered her. The fact their insistence on digging into her past and finding the man who fathered the girl was now threatening her marriage infuriated her.

"No, I've told you a hundred times, there's nothing that will embarrass you. You made sure before we married."

Somehow, David had gotten wind of an investigator looking into her background. He wouldn't tell her how, only that he was displeased and suspicious. Worry settled like a lead weight in her stomach. If there was one thing her husband had made clear before they married, it was his refusal to have anything to do with a woman with kids or someone who wanted children. While she'd been all for remaining childless, his attitude had surprised her. She figured men of his position and wealth all desired progeny to take over when they were gone. Instead, David was content letting his younger brother fulfill that goal, preferring an unburdened lifestyle.

She pivoted, and her gaze connected with Trey's as he entered the sunroom. Her blood surged at the angry glint in his eyes as he leaned against the wall with his arms crossed. He was supposed to have the week off, and his sudden appearance caught her at her most vulnerable, which was whenever her marriage was threatened. Trey did nothing to hide his protective displeasure when she and David argued, and, damn it, she loved that attention, more so now that she was over fifty. It was comforting to know at least one man cared for her, and desired her for more than appearances, even if she would never consider giving up her lifestyle and status for a relationship with a hired worker.

"Yes, dear, I hear you," she replied even though she'd missed David's last comment. "I'm well aware of that," she ground out, holding her temper back when he reminded her of their prenup. Turning from

Trey's glower, she sought to appease her husband. "Everything is set for the Carmichaels tonight. I hired Standford's to cater."

She'd gotten good at preparing for David to wine and dine his clients in their home. That was one area he often praised her efforts. "You're welcome. I'll see you later."

Constance ended the call then threw the phone in a fit of temper, not caring when it cracked against the wall. "Damn that woman!"

"Tell me," Trey insisted, and she never thought to do otherwise.

"I thought you were taking the week off."

He shrugged his broad shoulders, his gaze steady on hers. "I was on my way out until I heard you. What's going on?"

One night when David was out of town and she let the loneliness of her loveless marriage get to her, she'd sat in this very room, snuggled next to Trey on the wicker sofa. She'd already been well on her way to plastered when he'd joined her, and she'd spilled the beans about the pain of her former relationship. He'd been as incensed as she when the Flynns had dug up her identity.

"The Flynns hired yet another investigator, and his search has somehow reached David's ears.

I never should have given up trying to find someone willing to rid me of that kid instead of putting her up for adoption."

"You were young. Would Mr. Mayfield still hold that against you, even if she's now an adult?"

"Without a doubt," she returned with a bitter laugh. "It's baggage, whether in the past or present. Not only that, but I lied about it, which he'll say makes him look like a fool." Constance sank onto the sofa, the sun streaming into the room from the glass wall and skylights failing to warm her. "I wish to God that child didn't exist." Putting her head in her hands, she also wished Trey would comfort her, like he did that night. But he wouldn't put her at further risk by crossing that line again.

Trey Williams was the only honorable man she'd ever met, and she dreaded the day he tired of pining for a woman who cared more for materialistic trappings than she did any person, including him.

His shiny black shoes came into view as he stood before her then placed his hand on her bowed head. "Don't fret. Nothing will come of this, I'm sure."

Constance lifted her head and watched him walk out, wishing she could be as confident.

****

Mountain Bend

"Huh, my boss doesn't look happy. Go figure." Poppy grinned at Dakota as he turned onto the Bar S Ranch and she saw Jerry standing in front of his house, glowering.

"Yeah, go figure," he returned with a wry look.

"Better let me out here." As he pulled to a stop, she reached for the handle, but he stopped her from opening the door with a hand on her arm.

"I'll call you Wednesday or Thursday. Does that work for you?"

She could tell he was struggling with asking, or maybe he just found working on a relationship a chore. God knew she should be bored by now and thinking about moving on instead of where and how far they could go from here. "Yes, I'll make sure I get ahead on a few things to cut out early either day. I'm looking forward to riding Breeze, but remember, my riding skills are still rusty."

Dakota's face went tight, as if he were still working through the ramifications of what she'd gone through the past year. At least he hadn't dropped her like a hot potato when he'd heard the

C word.

"You'll do fine on her, as gentle as she is, despite her size. I'll stay alongside you." Reaching around her, he shoved the door. "Get some rest," he instructed, probably unaware he'd used that dominant tone she was now familiar with.

She couldn't help pushing him a little by answering with a two-fingered salute. "Yes, sir, Master Dakota." Hopping out of the Jeep, she kept her hand on the door as she turned to look back at him. "When my work is done, and *I* think I'm tired."

Shutting the door, she strolled toward Jerry without looking at Dakota again.

"Where have you been?" Jerry demanded to know.

Poppy regarded him for a moment, tickled by the show of concern on his face. "Safe and sound hanging out with your neighbor, but I appreciate that you were worried."

"*Hmmmph.* Just wondering if you were ever going to get to work. Now I can leave. I'll be gone until after lunch."

Jerry started toward his car in the driveway, but Poppy's curiosity wouldn't wait. She followed him, asking, "Where are you off to? I have time to run to town for supplies or anything else you need."

He hated going into town and had made it clear those trips were part of her job requirements.

"No problem. I'm meeting someone, so may as well get a few things while I'm there."

He moved fast when he wanted to and slid behind the wheel as she latched onto the door before he could shut it. "C'mon, give. Who...Betty? I heard someone mention her name when I noticed how chummy you two were at the picnic." She could tell by his face she was right, and she couldn't be more pleased. "That's great, Jerry. It's time you..."

"Don't go reading more into a simple lunch with my wife's friend than what it is," he snapped, tugging on the door. "We have more catching up to do is all. Close the damn door."

Poppy giggled and shut the door then leaned in the window to say, "Your neighbor and me? We're friends with benefits. I highly recommend it for you and Betty. I'm going in to get Otis. Have a good time." Like she did with Dakota, she turned her back and didn't glance around again as she dashed up to his front door and let Otis out.

Coming from the big city, she'd thought he was crazy for not locking his doors when he was gone. It hadn't taken her long to do the same once she'd discovered what little crime occurred around here. Lisa's stalker had been big gossip, from what she could gather, because nothing like that ever happened in Mountain Bend.

"Come on, boy," she called to the dog, hiking toward the cabin.

Each step emphasized lingering the soreness between her legs, a reminder of last night, this morning, and the common denominator between the two, Dakota. Not giving up on him had been worth the frustration and grief. She could still feel how his size had stretched her, filled her, and the tempered force of his fucking that drove her to a new euphoric high.

Yeah, no matter how tired and achy she was, with a whole day ahead of her yet, she admitted Dakota was worth every twinge. Now that her health issue was out in the open, she planned to enjoy him for as long as she could. Getting her fill of a man like him might take a while, for sure, longer than any of her previous lovers. For the first time, she found herself looking forward to a relationship instead of seeking a way to end one.

Poppy changed into work jeans and a soft cotton, short-sleeved pullover, going over what Dakota had said about his mother. His pain and anger over losing her in such a horrendous way, as well as his love for her, bled through in his voice. Her heart hurt for him, but she realized she had given more personal insight into her ordeal than him. He'd switched gears to sex so fast, she'd forgotten how deftly he had changed the subject.

The next time she saw him, she would let him know this wasn't going to be a one-sided give relationship instead of a give-and-take. Admitting she wanted more from him was now easy. How much more, she had yet to define and depended a lot on Dakota's willingness to meet her halfway.

"Let's go, Otis." She left the cabin, and Otis made a dash toward the pens, eager to work.

Poppy waved to Nathan and Mick, who were separating the sheep still waiting for shearing. Despite her lack of strength, she'd succumbed to the temptation to take a stab at the chore last week, grateful no one laughed at her clumsy fumbling. Mick jumped in to save both the ewe and her wool, as well as prevent Poppy from getting a painful whack from the angry sheep's hoof.

She would leave the final ones to the guys, deciding it was a younger, more fit person's chore. The rest of the morning she spent using her veterinary tech certification to tend wounds, most sustained by tangling with the barbed wire lining the top of some fencing or another sheep. Two new rams needed spraying for sheep ticks before she could turn them out with the rest of the flock, and she was keeping a close eye on a new mother and her premature lamb.

It was after four when Poppy called it a day and returned a tired, but happy Otis to his master then headed back to the cabin. The purr of a vehicle coming up the road behind her drew her head around, and, giving a pleased wave, she smiled at Lisa and Jen.

"What brings you out here?" she asked as they met up at the cabin.

"Curiosity about you and Dakota. Shawn mentioned seeing you with him early this morning, and inquiring minds can't wait for the lowdown." Lisa leaned against the car, Jen joining her and both wearing looks of expectation that hinted they weren't going anywhere without the juicy details.

Poppy realized she'd set down roots here in Idaho, starting with her friendships. When she didn't immediately start thinking about a change in jobs or mentally planning a long trip, she admitted she'd found something here, with the people, that was worth sticking around for, at least for the foreseeable future, or until something occurred to change her mind.

"Come on in, and I'll be happy to give you the juicy details. You look as tired as I feel, Lisa"

Following her inside, Lisa replied, "School's almost out for the summer, and the kids are wound up."

"Plus, she's leaving the end of the week for a trip to Phoenix, and her past," Jen added as they entered the cabin.

Poppy went into the kitchen and got down a glass, saying over her shoulder, "I forgot you mentioned that. Have you decided whether you'll answer your father's request to meet?" She and Lisa shared that in common, parents they never knew growing up.

"I don't know." Lisa's eyes reflected sadness and guilt. "I am responsible for his son's death, which would add to the awkwardness."

Jen frowned at her. "Shit, Lisa. You're no more responsible for that jerk's actions than you are that man's refusal to have anything to do with you before now. Like Shawn keeps telling you, you're under no obligation to ease his conscience now that he's old and alone."

Lisa shook her head. "Let's get back to Poppy and Dakota. If you tell us you spent the night at his place, you'll be the envy of half of Mountain Bend."

"*Oooh*, I've always wanted to be that woman everyone secretly resents. Take a seat." Poppy poured iced tea and set all three glasses on a plate to carry over to the table then retrieved a package of lemon cookies before taking a seat. "Help yourself," she offered, sliding the cookies over. "And yes, I spent the night in Dakota's bed, but the sex didn't happen until this morning, on the kitchen table."

Jen laughed, choking on her drink. "You crack me up," she gasped.

Lisa looked at her with an amused grin. "Oh, I won't be able to get that image out of my head for a while!"

"C'mon, you two. I've seen what goes on in that club. I've *participated* there. You can't be shocked by table sex." Poppy gabbed a cookie and took a bite. She loved lemon anything.

"No, not by that, by your blunt admission, given without a hint of embarrassment. Plus, to my knowledge, Dakota's never gotten involved with anyone outside of Spurs, at least, no one from around here," Jen said. "That's the real shocker."

"We're just screwing around. I wouldn't call that involved." At least, that's what she kept telling herself.

"Does he think that, too?" Lisa asked.

"How the hell does anyone know what he thinks?" Poppy returned with an edge to her voice she couldn't help because she wondered the same thing.

"You've got a point, but don't read anything into his closed mouth. A relationship is new territory for him," Jen advised.

"Since I'm unsure of my own feelings, that isn't a problem."

Lisa leaned forward with shining eyes. "New subject. Your boss, Poppy, and our Miss Betty. Word has it they were seen together again at the restaurant last night."

"I heard that." Jen nodded. "What did you say to bring about this positive change?"

Poppy put up her hands, as if warding off credit for Jerry and Betty's budding relationship. "All I did was mention the picnic, and that he should accept his friends' support. The rest is on them. Other than she was a good friend of Jerry's wife, I know nothing about this Miss Betty."

Lisa filled her in. "Betty Cooper, Buck's widow and Shawn, Clayton, and Dakota's foster mother. I've gotten close to her – it's hard not to – and she's a wonderful person."

"She must be if she could take on three teenage

boys," Poppy replied.

"I hope you're planning on staying. You're a good influence, even if it isn't by design." Jen finished her tea and stood. "But now I need to get back, if you're ready, Lisa."

"Ready. Thanks for letting us drop in unannounced, Poppy."

"I enjoyed our chat."

Poppy saw her friends off, determined to give all thoughts of Dakota a rest. That lasted while fixing a sandwich for dinner, playing chess with Jerry for two hours, and even through the night.

She awoke wondering what his plans were for the day, unable to deny a longing to hear his irritated voice, so much so, she threw herself into helping with the guys' chores instead of just supervising. Ending the afternoon spreading fresh hay in the horse stalls emphasized her sore muscles, and she put the pitchfork away with a sigh of relief. Grabbing a soda out of the small refrigerator in the break room, she walked to her porch, enjoying the quiet peacefulness that had settled over the farm after the hired hands departed.

Taking a seat on the rocking chair, she gulped the soft drink, not coming up for air until the rumble of truck tires reached her. When she recognized

Dakota's truck, her senses went on high alert before she recalled her sweaty, disheveled appearance.

"The heck with that," she muttered, forcing herself to stay put instead of dashing inside to clean up. She wasn't a young girl simpering over her first crush and wasn't about to hurry in, apply makeup and spritz on perfume before he saw her, even if her pulse went a little crazy at the prospect of seeing him again.

Poppy stayed seated, rocking, as Dakota stopped and slid out of the truck holding a large bag from the burger joint she'd only tried once on the day she bumped into him. Coincidence? She finished the soda, ignoring the rapid beat of her heart as she took in his sweat-dampened T-shirt, dirt-encrusted jeans, and, if she wasn't mistaken, a sign of manure on the side of his boot. Seeing evidence he'd come to her without much forethought, definitely no primping, hinted he might be fighting the same thing as her – how much she wanted to see him, be with him again. That he caved first titillated her in a way that had nothing to do with sex.

Dakota held up the bag. "Pete's running a special on double cheeseburgers."

Her mouth watered, from both the man and the aroma drifting from the bag as he joined her on the porch. "Do you want to eat out here or go inside?"

"Here. I ran into town right after working without cleaning up first." He folded his large frame onto the other rocking chair, and she almost laughed at his disgruntled expression.

"Hey, you picked out here," she pointed out.

"It's fine." Placing the bag on his lap, he reached over and plucked the can from her hand then pulled a bottled water from the bag and handed it to her. "Better for you."

"What about the greasy half-a-cow hamburger?" she teased, taking the wrapped burger. "Please tell me there are fries in there."

"You need the calories from the burger, and it's protein." Dakota pulled out a large fry and held it between them. "We'll share. Eat. I still have work to finish."

"Got it. Thanks." She unwrapped the burger and took a big bite, moaning as she chewed.

"Stop that," he ordered, glowering.

"Can't help it," she mumbled with her mouth full. "Didn't realize I was starving. Good."

He shook his head and downed his own sandwich before she finished. She eyed the movement of his thick, tanned throat as he drank, a coil of lust cramping her abdomen. Either that, or she ate too fast.

Poppy finished the last bite and snatched some fries while he stuffed the wrappers back in the bag.

"Here, you can finish them. Gotta run." Standing, he leaned over and cupped her nape, tilting her head up for a slow, thorough, demanding kiss. This time, she moaned into his mouth, and he pulled away with a curse. "Don't overdo tomorrow," he tossed out as he pivoted and strode back to the truck.

Giving a casual wave from behind the wheel, he left her with tingling lips, bemused, but pleased by the short, impromptu dinner.

****

Dakota rode into the stable yard and dismounted, waving Casey over. "Would you mind taking care of Blaze for me? I'm running behind." He held out the quarter horse's reins. Phantom always gave him the evil eye when he chose to ride one of the other horses, but he'd make it up to the stallion when they went out with Poppy.

"Sure thing, Boss. Do you need anything else?" Casey took the reins with a pat to Blaze's shoulder.

Lifting his hat, Dakota ran his fingers through

his hair, regretting losing the tie holding it back when it had slipped off. "Not unless I need to address something around here."

"We're good. The feedstore just made its delivery, and I've checked our inventory. Enjoy your outing."

Casey knew better than to rib him about the ride he planned with Poppy. He and a few other hands already had their fun this morning when he'd assisted with moving their largest herd up north now that warmer weather was here.

Replacing his hat, he nodded. "Thanks. Call me on the satellite phone if you need me." The extra expense of adding a way to communicate when cowboys were too far away to get cell service had come in handy calling for backup when Lisa's deranged half-brother had her and Shawn pinned down with gunfire. The stupid son of a bitch deserved the return fire from not only Shawn but Dakota and the ranch hands who had been close enough to ride to their rescue.

After sprinting into the house, he took a quick shower, recalling Poppy's worn-out appearance when he'd stopped by with the hamburgers. His first inclination had been to rail at her, but he'd stifled the urge to demand she stop pushing herself, which she would ignore. He was still adjusting to his uncharacteristic concern and protectiveness her past health ordeal had pulled to the surface. Prior to meeting Poppy, only his two closest friends, Miss Betty, and his mother possessed the power to call forth those emotions. Before staring into those blue eyes and seeing the undisguised mirth and lust she never attempted to shy away from, he'd thought himself immune to developing stronger feelings for anyone else.

It rankled to discover he could be so wrong about himself at his age. That didn't stop the faster beat of his heart when he finished showering and checked the time, seeing she would arrive soon.

Dakota dressed and padded downstairs, passing his office on the way to the kitchen. He hadn't had time to start a new search since discovering the last leads were more dead ends yesterday, but he would this evening, regardless of the turn in his relationship with Poppy. Just because he cared more than he'd expected didn't mean he would allow his growing feelings to interfere with his search for his mother's killer, even if his disappointment over the latest failure was less acute than ever before.

A fresh breeze wafted in from the open windows and back door, carrying the crunch of tires on the gravel drive followed by car doors shutting and low voices. He was expecting Miss Betty with the fried chicken he'd asked her to cook for today but wasn't surprised to see Clayton coming inside with her. If Shawn and Lisa hadn't left on their trip to Arizona, Dakota was sure they would have shown up with them.

"Why aren't you at work?" he questioned Clayton, leaning down to kiss the cheek Miss Betty turned up to him.

Clayton's casual shrug matched his tone. "I finished up early. Miss Betty and I are going to ride up to Quail Ridge."

Located alongside an eastern mountain range, Quail Ridge provided the idyllic spot for the Cooper family burials, high enough on the mountain slope to overlook the valley and shimmering lake below. They took turns tending the graves, including Buck's, and Dakota was glad Clayton made sure he accompanied Miss Betty, given his plans and Shawn's absence.

Giving them both a fond smile, she patted their faces. "Even though I'm not too old to ride up there on my own, I appreciate your thoughtfulness. And, Dakota, I couldn't be more pleased you have a girlfriend. We'll have to work on you next, Clayton."

They both jerked, their quick, simultaneous

replies refuting her comment.

"No way," Clayton insisted.

"She's not my girlfriend," Dakota denied.

Ignoring Clayton, Miss Betty kept her eyes lifted to Dakota and held up the plate of chicken. With a disgruntled sigh, he took the plate, muttering, "Fine, yes, she is. Thanks for the food."

"You're welcome, and don't worry, we're going straight to the stables. You can introduce me after we all return from our rides. Come on, Clayton."

Rolling his eyes as soon as she turned, Clayton gave him a silent thumbs-up and followed the woman who had grabbed their hearts the day they met. Dakota heard their foster mom say, "That nice girl Sharon Mize asked about you again when I had lunch at the Watering Hole," before the front door closed on Clayton's answer. Knowing what a sore subject the twice-divorced waitress was with Clayton ever since she'd refused to give up on him after they went out a few times, he didn't envy his friend's ride with Miss Betty. There wasn't much the three of them wouldn't do for her, but dating just to please her was one of them.

Another vehicle pulled up out front as he sealed the lid on the Tupperware he transferred the chicken to before grabbing two apples. Striding onto the porch, he decided the bright-red SUV suited Poppy, even if the color clashed with her hair. She met him at the bottom of the steps wearing an eager grin.

"I've been looking forward to this all day. Trail riding will be a new experience. Before moving here, I'd only ridden around the stable's acreage."

Balancing the apples on the chicken container, he clasped her elbow with his free hand. "The path we're taking is one of the most scenic on the ranch. Now that the bear we've been tracking is dead, I'm comfortable taking you that route."

"That's tragic, even if the animal is no longer suffering. Do you think the park rangers will find whoever was so careless?" she asked, her voice tinged with sadness.

He shook his head. "Doubtful, but Ben will keep trying."

As they approached the saddled horses, she flicked him a sly, teasing glance. "You know, if you ever want to plan another threesome, Ben's really hot." He couldn't help stiffening at that suggestion and, of course, she noticed. "I'm just saying."

Dakota released her arm to stuff the food in his saddlebag, keeping his face averted until the twist in his gut from her innocent remark loosened. If that reaction offered anything to go by, he'd guess another scene of sharing her was out of the question.

He surprised himself when he looked at her over Phantom's back and said, "Anything to do with sex is off the agenda today."

Disappointment flashed in her eyes but didn't linger. With a fine-by-me shrug, she quipped, "Sure. I didn't think you were the type to play risky where you work since you're the boss."

Frowning, he watched her mount Breeze without a hint of hesitancy about the mare's size. Considering his club ownership and involvement, he wondered whether she tossed that out as a challenge or honestly believed that nonsense. He swung up on Phantom then looked over in time to catch the gleam in her eyes and smirk playing about her lips.

He should have known. "I suppose telling you to behave is a waste of time."

Her laugh resonated in the air and drew several heads. Oblivious to the cowhands' interest, she tugged the reins from the rail, saying, "Let's go, Dakota. I promise not to leap across and jump your bones today. Is that good enough?"

"You'd break one of your foolish bones if you tried, which might be fun to watch if you keep pushing me. Phantom and Breeze have gotten acquainted, but ride close to me anyway, just in case you have trouble."

CHAPTER NINE

Poppy lied. The longer she rode next to Dakota with the sun warming her head and shoulders and his deep voice setting off those now familiar sparks of awareness, the more she longed to make that leap onto him. But first, she wanted him to fill in the blanks about his past. He'd kept the horses' gaits to a slow walk that provided an easy swaying rhythm to get into and maintain without much concentration. They trekked across a wide expanse of open rangeland dotted with a lavish array of golden-hued sunflowers interspersed with purple-blue Camas lilies, as well as other colorful spring wildflowers she wasn't familiar with. She could see the thin blue shimmer of a lake still too far away to detect the size, the mountains rising up behind it, and the black cattle enjoying a drink.

But the scenic landscape, perfect weather, and pleasant ride weren't powerful enough to keep her from aching for more of Dakota's dominant sexual expertise. She could easily label her infatuation lust if it weren't for the equally strong desire to learn more about his mother and his past, to hear from him how the Coopers had changed his life after that tragic loss. Lisa once mentioned he, Shawn, and Clayton had met in foster care, but Poppy sensed there was more to that story also, and, for the first time ever, she found herself interested in learning what made a man tick.

Then there were her uncharacteristic responses to a sexual lifestyle she'd sworn wasn't her thing until Dakota had put his hands on her. Was there more to this kinky stuff than she'd thought, or were those powerful orgasms just a strong reaction to the man who had intrigued her from the moment he'd appeared as a mysterious stranger out on a midnight run? Either way, the question begged for an answer, and the only way to get it was to continue exploring with him. That's how she saw it anyway.

Dakota pointed to a narrow path bisecting the woods off to their left. "Follow me through there. That leads to one of the streams I like to fish."

"Okay, but if fishing is on the agenda, you're on your own. I've never seen why I should pull the wriggly, slimy things from the water myself when I can buy them already skinned, deboned, and ready to cook, not to mention *already dead*," she emphasized.

Entering the forest, he turned his head and

scoffed. "City girl."

"Yep, and not planning on changing. Oh, it's nice in here."

The dense foliage provided cooler air and a closer look at small critters, such as squirrels, rabbits scampering about, and birds flitting from to tree to tree. They didn't talk until the path widened and she heard the gurgling flow of the stream.

"Here we are. If you're comfortable waiting to dismount until Breeze gets a drink, let her have the lead. If not, pull up and dismount," Dakota said when they rode into the open.

"I'm good." Poppy relaxed her grip on the reins, and Breeze walked to the stream's sloping edge, her front legs lower than her hind end as she dipped her head to drink. Leaning back to counterbalance the mare's awkward stance, she inhaled a deep lungful of fresh mountain air ripe with the scent of pine, sighing in relaxed pleasure. "Okay, this is nice."

"I thought you might enjoy this place. It's peaceful after a long day working." Dakota swung down as soon as Phantom quit drinking and moved back then dropped the reins to reach for the saddlebags.

"Won't he take off?" she asked, turning Breeze when she'd taken her fill.

"No, neither will Breeze if you do the same."

She alit, watching him pull a blanket from one saddlebag, and it dawned on her he'd planned a picnic. With tingling giddiness, she couldn't help ribbing him.

"Look at you, the big bad Dom going on an afternoon picnic. Who would guess?"

Dakota snapped the blanket out and laid it on the grassy ground, flashing her one of the annoyed glares that always amused her. Maybe because she was one of the few who could see he wasn't as put out as he liked to pretend.

"Do you want to eat or not? If so, you can always stand or sit on the ground with the bugs."

"And miss sitting close to you? I don't think so." Her stomach growled as she strolled over and sat down. "And I'm hungry."

Joining her, he handed her some napkins, opened the chicken, and held the container out. "Help yourself." When she only picked up a drumstick, he frowned. "Take at least two to start with."

"You're always shoving food at me," she said, taking a breast.

"Because you don't eat enough."

Dakota stretched one leg out and bent the other, resting his arm on his knee after biting into a large breast. She eyed the juices dripping down his chin with an urge to lick them then got sidetracked from that enticing idea when it dawned on her he was concerned after learning why she needed to put on a few pounds.

"You're taking care of me," she burst out, her heart somersaulting with surprise. And just like that, Poppy leaped over like and jumped straight into love.

His head snapped up, sending his hat upward to reveal his quick switch from instant denial to acceptance. That didn't stop him from lowering his dark brows in obvious dislike of her pointing out that fact.

"Shut up and eat, Poppy."

Chuckling, she lifted the chicken leg. "Yes, sir."

Given this change in their relationship, the confirmation he cared the same as her, Poppy broached the subject of his past as she finished the leg and started on the breast of the best fried chicken she'd ever eaten.

Savoring the crunchy, seasoned skin covering the moist meat, she kept chewing while asking, "How old were you when your mom died?"

Turning his gaze toward the stream, he was quiet for so long, she thought he wouldn't answer.

Then his tense shoulders relaxed, and he replied without looking away from the view. "Just shy of fourteen. I finished growing up fucking fast after finding her stabbed multiple times."

Nausea rolled through Poppy, the scene his words put in her head both horrifying and heartbreaking. Reaching out, she put her hand on his rigid forearm. "I'm sorry, Dakota. If you don't want to talk about it..."

"No, you need to know." He looked at her then, and she could see the raw pain reflected in his voice. "Up until that time, it was just the two of us. I didn't care because she was all I needed, the only person I ever loved. She moved off the reservation for me, saying the general public was more welcoming of mixed races than the pure-blood Indians of our tribe. She was right, but she hadn't figured in the higher cost of providing for us."

Poppy kept her tone neutral, which wasn't easy considering the empathy gripping her. "It must have been difficult, being a single mother with a growing boy who wanted to eat constantly." At least she got a rueful grin from him.

"I was already big by ten, so yeah, I think she saw what was coming. She worked hard, taking two jobs, pissing me off when she refused to let me mow lawns for extra money." He took several more bites, finishing the breast and reaching for another, his tone hardening as he said, "Then she took up with Vincent."

Poppy wiped her fingers and reached for the water bottle. "Is that who you think killed her?"

"No, that's who I know killed her. I saw him running from our apartment right before I returned and found her, and that's why I'll kill him when I find him."

His black eyes were chips of ice, and he didn't try to hide his anger from her any more than he had his intentions. A cold chill invaded her body, and she had trouble downing the water. The dead seriousness of his voice and reflected on his chiseled face scared her. Not that she feared for herself but for him if he ever found the man.

"You're willing to take that risk?"

She relaxed, watching a spasm of indecision cross his face, and hope shoved aside regret. She could never stay with someone who committed such an act, regardless of his reason.

"I'll know when I find him, won't I?"

Given what she'd first believed about him, what she knew now, and how she felt, she had to believe he would never go through with such an extreme revenge.

"Yes, I guess you will."

Poppy needed to get her mind off his disclosure and on to something else, something much more pleasurable before they headed back. He tilted his head to take a long drink of water, his bent leg emphasizing his thick quad muscle, not to mention pulling the denim taut through the crotch. She licked her lips, eyeing that bulge, enjoying all the lovely possibilities flitting through her head. Tracking her gaze up to his face, she encountered his heated look below his hat brim and decided the only thing sexier than a man wearing a Stetson was a man wearing *only* a Stetson.

A familiar fever rushed through her veins as she rose to her knees and crawled closer. His pulse jumped when she pressed her lips to the side of his corded neck, and she smiled against his warm skin.

"Do you know all the new things I've done since meeting you?" she asked without looking up. Lifting his hand off his knee, Dakota cupped her nape, his hold allowing only minimal movement for her to nibble, lick, and nip the left side of his neck.

"Like what?"

She loved his guttural tone that revealed his rising lust. "Like going to a kink club." She bit a prominent vein. "Cutting sheep from a cattle herd." She tongued the tender spot. "Getting restrained in said club." She pressed her lips to the underside of his chin. "Riding through the woods." She savored his indrawn breath. "Experienced the touch of two men." He squeezed her neck, and she gloated.

"Anything else?" he asked, allowing her enough movement to reach his mouth.

"Probably," she whispered against his lips. "But the only thing I can think of right now is what I haven't done." She sank her teeth into the lower one. "And want to more than I need my next breath."

"I doubt that," he drawled.

"Then, I guess I'll have to prove it to you."

Dakota released her neck, and Poppy wasted no time following the path she bared by unbuttoning his shirt down to his waist. His wide belt halted her progress but didn't deter her from her goal. With quick finger dexterity and determination, she undid the belt while teasing his naval with her tongue.

He cursed, returning his hand to her head as she carefully lowered his zipper over his raging erection. "I don't believe you've never done this before."

Poppy wrapped her fingers around his cock, shifting her eyes upward. "Never outdoors, and not at all with you."

"Then don't let me stop you from adding this to your list." With slight pressure, he urged her head downward.

Opening her mouth, she wrapped her lips around his mushroom cap, stroking the smooth skin, tasting his tangy seepage. He quickened in her grip, and she went hot, licking lower, stroking under the rim.

"Right there, baby," he rasped, trailing his hand around to run a finger over her lips.

Unable to resist, she included the tip of that finger in her next tongue swipe, satisfied with his groan. Inching down his thick length, Poppy swirled around his girth, teasing the protruding veins pumping his blood in a hot torrent responsible for warming his silk-covered flesh. It was her turn to groan as he grew harder, spewing more pre-cum. She went lower, engulfed more of his rigid shaft, her jaw already aching from his size stretching her cheeks. Stopping halfway, she pulled up with hard suction, tunneling her free hand under him to roll his sac in her palm.

Dakota surged upward, pumping into her mouth with slow, shallow dips, driving her as crazy as she hoped she did him.

****

Dakota's lust for Poppy was a greedy thing, clawing at his balls with a voracious need, hardening his cock into aching demand. With nature's music of twittering birds and the rapid flowing stream playing in the background, he watched her work her mouth on his cock as he pumped in and out. Her hand on his balls triggered the first contractions, and he sought to warn her.

"Back off unless you're into swallowing."

She ignored him, as he figured she would, and continued with her hot licks of pleasure until his orgasm erupted out of his cock in a fierce torrent of heat. Flames of pleasure tore through him as he pumped into her mouth, trying to remain gentle by gripping the base of his erection and preventing himself, and her, from going too deep with the dwindling convulsions.

When his head cleared of the euphoric fog, he handed his water bottle to Poppy as she raised her head. With a smile of gratitude, she drank the rest then said, "Looking out for me again? Thanks."

"It's in the Dom rules, somewhere." Unable to resist, he stood, pulling her up with him, and took her mouth in a deep kiss before adding, "Besides,

I'm starting to like taking care of you. Go figure."

"You can figure it out. I'll enjoy it while it lasts."

She turned from him before he could answer, and he let it go until he was sure of how far he wanted their relationship to go. "We'd better head back," he said, adjusting his jeans then taking her hand. She didn't hide how much she liked his hold, and he admitted he also enjoyed the simple intimacy he had never been inclined to undertake before.

They mounted and rode through the woods in silence then he faced her as they emerged. "Are you confident enough on Breeze to go for a run?"

"You bet," she returned without hesitation, her face suffused with excitement.

Liking her enthusiasm, he nodded. "Give her a light kick with your heels. She'll follow Phantom's lead. Hold on tight; keep your knees locked on her sides."

"Got it. Let's go."

Taking her at her word, they took off, starting with a trot until he was convinced she could handle a faster gait. With another nod, he called over to her, "One more kick, and we'll take off."

Poppy's gay laughter resonated across the pastureland as they raced, and Dakota couldn't help but grin in response, admiring her control, pleased she was showing signs of improved stamina. They arrived back at the stable breathless, and he found himself hard-pressed to remember when he'd enjoyed an afternoon or a woman more.

"That was a blast!" she burst out with a beaming smile and red face, reining Breeze to a halt.

"I'm glad you had fun," he answered, dismounting. "Need help with the saddle?"

"Nope. Got it."

They unsaddled the horses in silence then turned them into the corral before she gave him a regretful look. "I've got to get going. I promised Jerry a rematch on our last game. The final shearing is tomorrow, and I have to get up early."

There went his plans to invite her to stay the night. He'd never asked a woman to sleep over at his place, and the strong desire to have her in his bed again spoke volumes about where this was headed. Walking with her to her SUV, he realized he didn't have a problem with that.

Holding the door open for her, he ravished her mouth again, satisfied when her breathing accelerated. "I'll pick you up for the club tomorrow. Get plenty of rest tonight."

She sighed, shaking her head. "We need to work on this penchant you have for ordering instead of asking."

"Not if it has anything to do with getting you naked."

A rueful grin tugged at her lips as Poppy glanced down at her body then back up at Dakota. "Not that I'm not thrilled with getting hot and sweaty with you again, but given you can have just about anyone, are you sure? I'm still practically boobless and too thin."

"I'm sure. And you're not boobless." He squeezed her breast to show her she was a pleasant handful. "You are too thin." He swept a hand down her body and palmed one soft buttock. "But you have a great ass."

"I do?" Pleasure colored her voice, and she leaned into him. "'Cause I'm just saying. Take that one girl with the big boobs who looks soft and cushy where I'm not and is always coming on to you."

"You fuck her, then. Kathie comes on to everyone, so maybe she'll go for a little girl-on-girl action."

Poppy responded to that suggestion with a low laugh and calculated gleam in her blue eyes. "I would but I really" – she caressed his shoulders – "really" – then glided downward to press against his chest – "like hard more."

Taking her shoulders, he urged her down

onto the driver's seat. "And I like all female shapes, including skinny." Shutting the door, he leaned into the open window and yanked on her short curls. "See you tomorrow night."

The next day, Dakota had just knocked off work and entered the house when a call from Clayton halted him halfway to the shower. "What's up?" he asked, more interested in getting to Poppy's cabin than talking to his friend.

"Trouble at the club. Can you get here ASAP?"

Fuck. Pivoting, he strode back out as he replied, "On my way. What happened?"

"Break-in, back door, and from the hard-to-notice professionalism, by someone who knew what he was doing."

While there was never a shortage of negative comments and those who would like to see Spurs shut down, neither Randy, the previous owner, nor the three of them had suffered a destructive attempt on the building.

"Could be random, thugs looking to rob the place or kids seeking thrills." If it was someone from Mountain Bend, teens were the likely culprits.

"I've never known either to be this careful. I'll be inside."

Before Dakota could tell Clayton to wait for

him, he clicked off, and Dakota swore, stomping on the gas. As he approached the turnoff to the Bar S entrance, he saw the car driving toward him in the opposite lane slow then pull to the side. Passing him at a reasonable speed, Dakota couldn't make out much of the man behind the wheel except he was turned toward Sanders' place. As Dakota passed and continued watching the car in his rearview mirror, he eyed the driver getting back on the road then making a U-turn and executing a slow drive-by, his head again turned toward the sheep ranch as he passed.

Tense with suspicion, Dakota accelerated, making a mental note to warn Sanders once he returned and could look up his number. He parked next to Clayton's Bronco and hurried inside, stepping in the water covering the foyer floor.

"What the hell?"

Clayton appeared in the open door to the club room and waved him inside. "I've shut the water off. Wait until you see in here."

Walking into the room, fury shook him at seeing the overturned equipment, broken glass, and busted chairs and tables. They toured the damage together, Dakota's disgust at the vandalism rising with each infraction.

"If it's kids, I'll take a switch to them myself," he threatened.

Clayton's usual mild manner had been replaced with cold determination. "I'll help you. But if it's adult thugs, I get the pleasure of seeing to it they are locked up for an exceedingly long time."

"But I get to watch."

"You bet."

Ben and Simon arrived, followed by Kevin, a deputy sheriff from the same office in Mountain Bend as Shawn. Dakota could imagine how pissed Shawn was going to be when he and Lisa returned from Phoenix.

"Son of a bitch!" Ben exclaimed as Simon clenched his jaw and ground out, "Fuckers."

Kevin pulled out a notepad and started writing and talking at the same time. "Now that we've got that out of our systems, let's get to work. Needless to say, you won't be opening tonight."

Clayton pulled out his phone. "I'll send a membership text."

"We'll start mopping up after Kevin takes his photos." Ben and Simon returned to the foyer where the storage room was located near the restrooms.

Dakota sent a quick message to Poppy, regretting the delay in seeing her again the most.

It was just after ten by the time they finished cleaning up, the dumped liquor all over the bar and floors taking the longest to clear away. Everyone examined the back door and agreed the lack of obvious damage and fingerprints ruled out kids and pointed the finger at an experienced thief. Their best guess was he, or they, were looking for cash and had let loose with their anger when they had come up empty. Money was never held over at the club for that very reason.

"Let's call it a night, guys," Kevin suggested after they'd completed a final inspection. "That's all we can do for now. You might want to consider remaining closed tomorrow night."

"Already done. There's not time to restock the liquor and replace the busted furniture. The damage to the equipment is all minor from hitting the floor with impact, but to ensure everything is still stable, let's get them fixed." Clayton narrowed his eyes to slits as they walked out. "I can't wait to get them in court."

"Translation," Dakota put in, "find them fast, Deputy Sheriff."

"We'll do our best but could use Shawn's help," Kevin returned.

"He'll be back soon," Clayton assured him.

Dakota waved and went to his truck, tired and pissed but still wanting to spend time with Poppy. He'd called earlier and let her know he would be at the club cleaning up for a while, and she insisted he call when they were done, regardless of the time. The concern in her voice and picturing her curled next to him again in his big bed tempered his anger.

Grabbing his phone as he followed Clayton, he sent her a quick text, saying he was on his way. No sense in her getting out to meet him at his place when he was already so close to hers. Her quick answer of *I'm waiting* had him picking up his speed as soon as he turned onto the main road.

When he reached Sanders' place, he dimmed his headlights to avoid the sudden glare hitting a window in either the house or Poppy's cabin. Sanders didn't need to know and wouldn't mind him on his property this late considering his relationship with his manager, and said manager was expecting him. As he neared the cabin, his skin prickled with a sudden wave of unease. Hoping it was a cautionary reaction due to the recent vandalism at the club, he heeded the odd warning and slowed to a crawl so he could search around the cabin for any sign of trouble.

Dakota went rigid, spotting it in the form of a

man creeping toward the back. A cold infusion of fury and fear for Poppy spread through him as he came to a stop and inched out of the truck without shutting the door all the way to avoid any noise. He was fucking good at tracking in silence and followed the intruder with the grim purpose of exacting retribution for attempting to scare and/or harm his girl.

Yeah, she's my girl, and perfect for me. Admitting that added to his building rage over this threat to her as he peered around the side to catch the bastard inching to the back. Waiting until he disappeared, Dakota crept along the log side, pausing to sneak another peek around the corner when he reached the back. The man was so focused on breaking into the window Dakota guessed led into her bedroom, he never turned from his task as Dakota snuck up behind him with all the stealth his Indian DNA gifted him with.

Satisfaction struck like a bolt of lightning as he snaked an arm around the man's throat and heard his surprised gasp and desperate struggle for air. His hands clawed at Dakota's forearm as he attempted to kick one foot behind Dakota's leg to take him down. Sidestepping the maneuver, he chuckled in the intruder's ear, tightening his hold.

"I see you're an experienced fighter. But when it comes to threats against someone I care about, I fight dirty." Without a qualm of remorse, Dakota squeezed his windpipe until he slumped, passing out from lack of air. He dropped him to the ground as a light appeared in the window, followed by Poppy's pale face etched with terror. For that alone, he could easily snap the man's neck.

Shoving up the window, she looked down, frowned, then her eyes rose to check Dakota over. "He's still breathing, isn't he?"

"Yes. You okay?"

Relief spread across her face, and a small smile replaced her worry. "My hero, yes, I'm fine. I've called 911, and there they are," she said as the wail of sirens approached the front. "You're keeping the sheriffs busy tonight."

"Which makes these two incidents too much of a coincidence to ignore. Go get the door while I drag this son of a bitch out to them."

Kevin and two highway patrol officers came forward to take his burden from him as soon as Dakota reached the front of the cabin. Sanders stood talking to Poppy on the porch, gesturing wildly then glaring at him. Slapping handcuffs on the culprit who was starting to rouse, Kevin looked from Sanders to

Dakota.

"I think he blames you for this disturbance."

"I'll set him straight."

Kevin nodded to the other two officers who held the man by his arms even though he was awake enough to stand on his own and his hands were cuffed behind him. "Can you wait a minute, and I'll ask Ms. Flynn if she recognizes him?"

"Is that necessary tonight?" Dakota snapped, not wanting to put her through anything else tonight. He gave the large man his scariest glare, but he didn't flinch, just maintained his cold-eyed stare of indifference. He would wager Breeze's first foal the guy was ex-military.

"Yes, Dakota, it is," she said behind him. Placing a hand on his arm, she looked at the man who stared back with a blank gaze. Shaking her head, she said, "Sorry. I've never seen him before."

"Okay, thanks." Kevin tipped his hat to them then turned to the officers. "I'll follow you to the station."

"See you there, Deputy Sheriff," the oldest one replied before tugging on the man's elbow to get him moving.

"Question his whereabouts earlier, would you?" Dakota asked Kevin. "I'm guessing our break-in was to keep us busy and Poppy home tonight." Which would have worked if he hadn't needed to see her and be with her again.

"My same thoughts, but it's doubtful he'll say much, if anything. Not until a lawyer can get there. Good night."

"I'll check in with you tomorrow, Kevin. Thanks." Reaching for Poppy's hand still holding onto his arm, he squeezed her fingers as Sanders met them at the foot of the porch steps.

"Tell me you're staying the night," he demanded, the porch light revealing his concerned look.

"Better. I'm taking her home with me."

"Oh, really?" She tried tugging from his grasp but failed. Narrowing her eyes, she opened her mouth to argue, but he placed a finger over her lips, stopping her.

"I'll sleep better with you away from the cabin until the cops return in the morning to gather evidence."

"You could have started with that." Regret replaced annoyance in her tone as she told Sanders, "I'm sorry for the disturbance, Jerry."

"Got my heart pumping, that's for sure. Stay the weekend. I'll call if I need you."

He all but stomped toward his house, his gruff

response failing to mask his worry. Dakota could appreciate the effort.

"Come on, Poppy. I'll help you grab a few things, and we'll get out of here for a while."

CHAPTER TEN

Poppy sat in one of Dakota's porch chairs watching Clayton try to keep his seat atop a bucking bronco. She admired his stamina and lean, muscled body working to control the unhappy stallion. He'd already taken two tumbles but had gotten right back up on the horse who eyed him with distaste. With a loud *whoop* of success, the prosecutor brought the mustang to heel, his arm muscles rippling with his tight grip on the reins while his mount now revealed his displeasure by galloping around the enclosure with wild tosses of his head.

She checked the time, grateful for the entertainment to distract her from waiting for Dakota to finish talking to Deputy Sheriff Kevin. In all her years living in Houston, she'd never been victimized. The attempted break-in at the cabin last night left her on edge, and she didn't like it one bit. There was nothing to fret about since Dakota had arrived in time to thwart the stranger's plans, whatever they were. The best part of his intervention was confirming what she'd believed all along – he didn't have it in him to commit cold-blooded murder. She didn't doubt for one second he would kill someone in self-defense, or in defense of others, and the culprit left him no choice.

Her big bad Dom possessed a protective gene toward those he cared about, and she counted herself lucky she was one of them, even if he'd never admitted it aloud. She'd woken this morning to his low, rumbling voice assuring Shawn she was fine after relating the details in a harsher tone. He took a call from Betty as soon as he clicked off from Shawn, his voice turning warmer as he explained both he and Poppy were okay. Poppy stayed under the covers, smiling until the peal of her phone forced her to come out. Then, it had been her turn to calm her friend Jen and convince her they were both fine.

She smiled now, thinking about the pros of small-town living. For the life of her, she couldn't come up with a single con.

Clayton dismounted from the now-subdued stallion, both of them winded. Snatching up his hat off the ground, he plunked it over his sweat-dampened blond hair, a boyish grin of success splitting his rugged, tanned face. She could really go for him if she weren't so crazy stupid over Dakota.

Speaking of Dakota. Poppy swiveled her head as he came out of the house looking unhappy. "Kevin didn't learn anything," she said, assuming that was the reason he walked toward her with a look that said he was worried about upsetting her.

"He did, just not a lot." He squeezed her shoulder and remained standing instead taking the chair next to her. "His name is Trey Williams, and he works for your mother, your birth mother," he clarified when she frowned. "He claims she knows nothing of his trip here, and that he acted alone. Why, he's not saying, but the sheriff came in and is contacting the Houston authorities to talk to her."

Poppy winced. That was going to go over like a lead balloon. "I'd better call my parents and warn them."

"They aren't in danger, Poppy."

"I know, but, against my wishes, they insisted on hiring someone to find my birth parents, hoping one would agree to get tested and prove a match for another bone-marrow transplant. The odds of success are exponentially higher with a familial donor, but Constance Mayfield returned their letter, telling them I was their responsibility and not to contact her again."

She looked up and flashed him a quick grin, seeing his scowl. "Oh, it gets better. She agreed to meet my mom when she contacted her again, this time threatening a lawsuit my parents can't afford if her wealthy husband ever got wind of my existence. Apparently she went to great extremes keeping my birth a secret to land a wealthy husband who wanted nothing to do with kids. My parents' desperate pleas fell on deaf ears, their request a threat to her cushy lifestyle."

"Fucking bitch." He moved away from her to pace the porch. "If she didn't send her goon after you, she's somehow responsible. She has to be, as it's the only thing that makes sense."

Poppy agreed but kept quiet. He was pissed for her enough already; she didn't need to add fuel to the fire.

He stopped pacing and leaned against the rail, crossing his arms. The emotions swirling in the black depths of his eyes added to the bad-boy image his usual black shirt, Stetson, snug denim, and scuffed boots portrayed.

"What about your father – sorry, your birth father?"

She waved an airy hand. "I call him my sperm donor, when I have to call him anything, and that's my parents' current quest. I'm hoping they'll drop it once I tell them about last night."

"They love you."

His acute insight didn't surprise her; he'd read her easily enough. "Yes, they do, as much as I love them. Which is why I don't want them going through their savings on these endless searches that can lead to bad consequences instead of good. I'm fine now, and another match will turn up someday."

"With no guarantee it will stick," he returned, frowning.

Poppy shrugged, ready to change the subject. "There are no guarantees in life except death." Pushing to her feet, she said, "I'm going in to call them, then I want to do something other than talk about last night or my health."

Dakota's gaze softened, and he nodded. "When you're done, you can come with me to pick out a puppy. I need another herding dog, and there's a new litter of Australian Shepherds at a neighboring ranch you can help me choose him from."

Pleased with the invitation to such a fun outing and chance to view a new litter of puppies, she exclaimed, "I'd love to!" then rushed forward and hugged those broad shoulders, her pulse leaping as he squeezed her tight in return. "Can we bring her back today?" she asked as soon as he released her.

"No, *he's* only two weeks old." He glanced toward the steps, a rueful twist to his mouth seeing

Clayton's dusty appearance. "Who won?" he asked dryly.

Clayton's look turned smug. "I did, of course."

Poppy slipped inside, leaving them to bullshit each other while she called home. Her dad answered on the first ring, sounding excited.

"Your timing is excellent, sweetheart. We just heard from our investigator."

Poppy sank down onto the den sofa with a sigh. "I was hoping to talk you into dropping his search."

"No way, not now. He's found your birth father, and you have a twenty-four-year-old half-sister. Your mom is penning a letter right now, and we'll send it overnight delivery, but since tomorrow is Sunday, it won't arrive until Monday. Fingers crossed!"

Poppy wasn't excited. The odds of either of these strangers agreeing to get tested, let alone go through the transplant process for her were minimal at best. She knew nothing about Constance Mayfield's relationship with this man and didn't care. They had their chance to be her parents and threw it away. As for learning she wasn't an only child, that might thrill her under normal circumstances. She didn't need the disappointment of her rejection to intrude on her new relationship with Dakota.

"Dad, please don't get your hopes up. Have you

and Mom talked about coming up here for a visit?"

"A little, but let's wait to hear back from them first. With luck, you'll be returning soon."

Since there was no point in arguing, she let it go and spent a few minutes talking with her mother before hanging up.

****

Poppy's warm, naked body slid sensuously on top of Dakota in the dark. Her breathy moan against his neck increased the feverish blood flow engorging his cock. Wondering if she was even awake, he kept quiet and coasted his hands down her smooth back to cup her soft buttocks. He liked the weight she'd put on since they'd first met and intended to see she kept it up until she reached her previous weight. Her past suffering bothered him but not as much as the possibility of her having to go through it all again.

"Dakota," she whispered against his chest, right before she licked one nipple and sent tingles racing down to his already inflamed groin.

"Keep that up, and this will end before you get it started," he warned, squeezing her ass.

Her chuckle against his other nipple went straight through him. "Wouldn't want that." She gifted that nub with one tongue swipe then rose above him to grip his hips with her knees.

Dakota held his breath, letting her fumble on the bedside table for a condom with only the white illumination from the moon shining in the window to see by. He let her sheath his cock without taking over like he wanted, even though he owed her a retaliation for sweet-talking him into a female puppy. There was time for that after he gave her these few moments first.

As soon as she finished covering his rigid flesh, she gripped the base and held tight as she lowered herself, enveloping his cock in her snug, slick pussy one slow inch at a time. Gritting his teeth, he suffered through the press of her hands on his chest for balance as she rode his shaft with undulating sensuousness of her pale body. When her breathing quickened, along with her movements and tightening inner muscles, he took over.

"My turn, baby."

Lifting her off him, Dakota flipped her onto her stomach then yanked up her hips. In one smooth thrust, he was nestled back inside her pussy, relishing the immediate clamp around his cock. Holding onto her left hip, he finished what she started with pounding strokes and butt slaps, the room echoing with their carnal fucking, his heavy pants, and her soft, mewling cries.

Poppy's pussy sucked his climax from his balls within seconds, her tight convulsions failing to slow his ramming plunges as he let go with a guttural groan of pleasure. Despite still rippling around him as he pulled out of her, she was lowering her hips and asleep again before he caught his breath.

After disposing of the condom, Dakota slipped back into bed again, unable to think of a better way to wake in the middle of the night.

Wednesday morning, Dakota rose at the crack of dawn, like usual, thinking about talking to Poppy about moving in with him. It was a big step for both of them, given her strong independent nature and his aversion to commitment while he still sought his mother's killer. He went over the pros and cons while dressing and eating breakfast, and the only negative he could come up with was the hole in his gut from failing to avenge his mother's death.

"Speaking of which," he muttered, hearing the computer alert signaling his search had found something as he carried his empty plate to the sink.

He knew better than to hope this was it, the end to his labors and the beginning of his retribution but couldn't prevent the adrenaline surge that picked up his step into the office. Taking a seat, he pulled up the results and went cold.

"Fuck it, I've got you, you motherfucker." He stared in stunned disbelief at the photo in front of him.

The man was older than the last time he'd seen him, but there was no mistaking this was the same Vincent who had ended his affair with his mother by stabbing her to death. Dakota didn't need to do an advanced search to know for sure, but he started one anyway before reading through the biography, his tense body vibrating with emotion. When he reached the date Vincent had moved his family overseas to Switzerland, he realized why it had taken so long to find him. He should have figured the weasel would run away to the safety of a place known to refuse extradition.

Vincent Pasquino had lived a cushy life up until last year when his wife and daughter were killed in a car accident. *Too bad it couldn't have been him.* Dakota stood, dismissing that thought. For twenty long years, he'd craved ending that man's life with his own hands, watching his eyes as he told him who he was, and why he was going to die. It was the only thing that had kept him sane those first few years after losing his only parent. Once the rage that threatened to consume him dwindled to despondent anger, his searches, planning, and plotting kept him grounded. Working toward his goal of avenging her eased the pain of her horrific death; knowing he'd never stop prevented him from going off the deep end.

And now, at long last, he could put his well-thought-out plans into action. For some reason, Vincent had returned to Phoenix a few weeks ago, maybe to live out whatever time he had left in his home state. Given he was already past seventy and appeared frail, Dakota doubted he had a lot of years left. That didn't change his mind, and, while the computer did its thing, he made plane reservations and went over what to tell Shawn, Clayton, and Poppy.

****

"Mom, I'm busy. Can I call you back?" Poppy brushed the back of her hand across her damp forehead, watching the small ewe scamper back to the flock. That was her second attempt to check the wound she'd seen on the sheep yesterday. At least the ewe had cooperated enough for her to make sure it was a minor cut that didn't need a dressing. She'd wanted to get that done before she called it quits for the day, and she was supposed to meet with Jerry after the final shearing this afternoon.

"Poppy, you'll never guess what!"

Smiling at her mother's enthusiasm, she mouthed a thank-you to Mick, who held the gate open for her while she asked, "What?"

"She's a match!"

Frowning, Poppy picked up her step as she left the pen area and started back to the cabin. "Who's a match for what?"

"Your sister, half-sister. The first thing she did when she got my letter was get her HLA checked then she called. She wants to meet you."

Stunned at this sudden news, Poppy clutched the phone tighter and stopped walking. "Just like that? She's not even skeptical about your letter?"

"Nope. Her father confirmed his relationship with Constance Mayfield, and that she'd been pregnant with a girl when they split. MD Anderson already has her test results. When can you leave?"

Before now, Poppy had refused to let herself hope for a successful transplant. It was easier to stay convinced her cancer would remain in remission if she didn't dwell on finding a right donor again and hoping the second time would stick. She wasn't sure if the tremors of excitement dancing around inside her were due to hearing she had a sister or because of a stranger's quick, willing response to a plea from someone she'd never met.

"I'm not sure, possibly tomorrow," she answered, thinking of all she had to do before she left for possibly weeks, depending on how fast she recovered enough to finish convalescing here. The procedure itself could be done within a week of testing and took anywhere from ten minutes to a few hours. But the recovery time took anywhere from months to years. Her whirling thoughts jumped to Dakota and the impact on their budding relationship this would have. "Let me talk to my boss and get back to you, Mom."

She said goodbye and dashed inside to clean up and change before talking to Jerry then heading to Dakota's. She hadn't seen him in three days, her mind occupied the whole time with intruding thoughts about returning to his ranch, and his bed, hoping he wouldn't make her wait until the weekend. This news gave her a reason to drive over and surprise him.

An hour later, with Jerry's blessing and promise to hold her job until she returned from Houston and her enthusiasm to meet her sister and undergo another transplant skyrocketing, she drove through the entrance to the Rolling Hills Ranch, buzzing with an adrenaline rush of anticipation. From the interest and concern he'd exhibited since hearing about her treatments, she couldn't believe he would be anything but happy for her.

As his house came into view, some of her elation dwindled seeing the sheriff's cruiser and another vehicle parked in front. Shawn and Clayton came out the front door with Dakota as she got out, their faces reflecting displeasure and concern.

Coming down the steps, Shawn snapped, "See if you can talk some sense into him."

Clayton gave her a look of sympathy and squeezed her shoulder, following Shawn to their vehicles. As soon as they pulled out, she turned to Dakota, who spoke before she could even say hello, his words sending a cold chill down her spine.

"I found him, Poppy. The man who killed my mother."

"And?" she said, afraid by the icy determination stamped on his face she knew the answer.

He crossed his arms, his stance and voice implacable. "I leave first thing in the morning."

With her heart crumbling, she walked slowly up the steps, stopping in front of him, aching to hold him and erase the haunted pain in his dark eyes. "To do what?"

He swore, spun around, and strode inside. Poppy sighed and followed, deciding not to impart her own news. This was a decision he had to make without her influence. Given the time and effort he'd spent to find this person, and his grief, he would need to realize what he was planning was as wrong as the crime this man had committed, and that no amount of satisfaction from revenge would alter the past. Their relationship was too new for her to think he would put her news before executing his long-awaited plans.

That saddened her in more ways than one.

"To end his miserable existence," Dakota replied, closing the door behind them. "Can you stay tonight? I don't leave for the airport until after nine."

Poppy remained by the door and shook her head, a heaviness spreading across her chest as she sidestepped his reach for her hand. She'd gotten comfort from his possessive hold before, but the tight clasp of his larger hand around hers wouldn't help her despondency over his intentions.

"No, I can't. Shawn and Clayton didn't look happy with you."

His mouth turned down, and regret flashed

across his face. He cared about his friends and maybe her to a lesser extent. She would love it if he cared enough to put her above his revenge. *I love him,* she thought, closing her eyes, her stomach clenching. Too bad the first time for that life-changing happening occurred with this man, at this time in their lives, when he was hell-bent on throwing away the rest of his life.

"I know, but I have to do this. You can't stay, or won't?"

Opening her eyes, Poppy saw he'd crossed his arms again, his face as hard as his tone. "Won't. I'm sorry, Dakota." Fumbling for the door handle behind her, she opened it, saying, "I hope you'll change your mind. Goodbye."

****

Those were the same words Shawn and Clayton had said to him, and Dakota experienced the same stab of pain hearing them come from Poppy in the same subdued, regretful tone. The hurt and disappointment that had dimmed her bright-blue eyes bothered him. Most women worked at shielding their feelings, but not Poppy. From the moment she'd bumped into him at the feedstore, she'd done nothing to keep her thoughts or emotions in check. And damn it, he liked that about her. It was a refreshing change from the women he usually associated with.

An uncomfortable vise squeezed his chest as he turned from the door and went to finish packing. His feelings since finding Vincent had been all over the fucking place, so much so, he couldn't make heads or tails of them; whereas, before the photo appeared on his computer, he'd been dead sure about what he'd do when he dug up the right man. He didn't lack confidence in his decision-making and wasn't someone who questioned himself or his actions often. That he was doing so now, after all the years of surety over the course he'd set for his retribution, rankled him.

Dakota refused to dwell on Poppy, Shawn, and Clayton's obvious discontent with him and finished the day prepping to leave, mentally going over his plans for when he reached Phoenix. He had Vincent's address and would need time to scope out the place for the easiest and safest way to get inside. Just imagining Vincent's shock upon seeing him gave him a thrill of satisfaction, and he couldn't wait to see the look on his face when he realized why he'd come.

At long last, he would keep his vow to avenge his mother.

Phoenix, four days later

For the third evening in a row, Dakota sat in his rental car, keeping vigilance on Vincent's upscale house, wondering what the fuck was holding him back. After arriving Thursday, he'd found the right address but had returned to his motel room to get a good night's rest before confronting him. That was the first part of his plan to go awry, as he'd failed to sleep any better that night than the previous, a repeat of tossing and turning with plaguing memories of times with his mother, his friends, and the past weeks since meeting Poppy. He'd awoken with the urge to visit Father Joe, which pissed him off because the last thing he needed was a sermon, and the good priest knew of his search for Vincent, just not why he wanted to find him.

All of their faces kept popping up in his head, each reflecting concern, disappointment, and love. Even Poppy's. He couldn't figure out if he'd imagined that heart-twisting sentiment in her gaze since no woman had ever looked at him that way. Given she'd turned around and walked away, saying goodbye as if she'd meant it for good, he decided his head was screwing with him because he missed her. He'd discounted that option the first day, considered it the second, dwelled on it the third, and today was forced to admit the truth.

For the first time in his life, he was pining for a woman, aching to hear her voice, see her quirky smile that used to annoy him, enjoy her standing up to him, needing her to ease the lust only she could sate.

So why wasn't he slipping inside Vincent's house as soon as darkness descended, exacting his retribution, and hightailing it home to work at getting her to understand why he had to do what he had to do? Sitting out here for hours, doing nothing more than remembering the past and the people who had impacted his life the most since that fateful night, had been as far as he'd gotten in his quest. He needed to act soon, tonight, or go home.

The thought of failure twisted his gut into knots.

Dakota's phone beeped with an incoming text the same moment the double wrought-iron gates to Vincent's house swung open. Not seeing anyone, he reached for his phone, surprised to see the message was from Shawn. He hadn't heard from him or Clayton since Thursday. Taking the time to read it, he jerked at the news Shawn's short message imparted.

Poppy's in Houston, prepping for a bone-marrow transplant tomorrow.

What the hell? Why hadn't she said anything? He should be there with her, would have been if... then he remembered the excitement on her face when she'd slid out of her SUV, and how fast it had disappeared, replaced with disappointment when he'd told her without even greeting her that he'd found Vincent. She'd kept quiet after hearing his news, and, if he were to guess, she'd been hoping he would choose her over his revenge. Fuck, he couldn't have screwed up worse if he tried.

A car came up the street and turned through the gate, and his whole body went taut with expectancy, coldness filling him at the prospect of confronting his mother's killer after all this time. Dusk had fallen, leaving enough natural light added to the exterior house lights for him to get a good look at the younger man who had been driving as he got out and opened the back door.

With no thought in mind, Dakota left the obscurity of his car to lean against the closed door.

His whole body vibrated with suppressed emotion watching the other man assist frail, stooped Vincent Pasquino from the car, yet he couldn't get the image of Poppy lying in a hospital bed out of his head. Leaning heavily on a cane, aided by the IV bag attached to a stand that he gripped with his other hand, Vincent's poor health was obvious. Dakota reached a startling conclusion, staring at his twenty-year obsession – he was more moved by Poppy's plight than by imagining Vincent dead.

Dakota's heart pounded double-time, his palms going damp as Vincent looked up and spotted him. His lips moved, shock followed by dread spreading across his lined face, no doubt recognizing Dakota. But instead of going over his plan to end the man's miserable existence, all he could think about was Poppy undergoing that treatment without him, maybe suffering another rejection in the upcoming weeks, of the teasing glint in her blue eyes replaced with disappointment, her usual, upbeat persona dragged down by another failure or because she thought he didn't care enough to be there, supporting her. That possibility made him swear, his hatred of Vincent escalating as he blamed him for the rift between himself and Poppy and the hurt he'd inadvertently caused the woman he loved.

Dakota went light-headed with that admission, and suddenly *nothing* was more important than going to her. Without wasting another minute on the old man struggling to keep his composure in face of his fear, he pointed a finger at Vincent then turned his hand to aim two fingers toward his eyes before pointing both back at Vincent. His face paled at the implied threat, and Dakota was surprised at the satisfaction he experienced knowing the murdering bastard would live whatever time he had left quaking in fear. Now, when he thought of his mother and Vincent, he could imagine the old man's mental suffering, looking over his shoulder the rest of his life, wondering when Dakota would return.

He had one more stop to make before he changed his ticket and flew to Houston. Dakota got back behind the wheel, resigned to driving away from his revenge but content with the new purpose taking its place – Poppy.

Twenty minutes later, he rapped on Father Joe's door, not even sure why he felt the need to stop here before going to the airport. He hadn't told anyone about this trip except Shawn, Clayton, and Poppy. All he told his foreman was he'd been called out of town for a few days. He'd almost called Miss Betty but couldn't bear to lie to her or tell her the truth.

"Dakota! What a nice surprise." Father Joe held the door open, beckoning him inside. "Why didn't you tell me you were coming?"

"It was a spur-of-the-moment trip."

The small rectory hadn't changed much over the years. The same sofa he'd sat on that night over twenty years ago when Shawn had led them here still faced the television, which was a newer flat screen. The compact kitchen sported new countertops and appliances, but the coffee pot and toaster still sat in the same spots.

"Sit down, son. What can I get you?"

Dakota turned to look at him, a man much shorter than himself, with wire-framed glasses and thinning gray hair. The priest and Buck were the only men he'd allowed to call him son, figuring they'd earned the right as the only men in his life who had stood by him no matter how much grief he gave them. Father's expression remained calm, even serene, but the shrewd look in his eyes didn't miss a thing. He didn't realize how much he was counting on that until Father spoke again.

"Or would you rather talk?"

Dakota blew out a breath and started pacing the wood floor. He surprised himself when he blurted,

"I found Vincent."

Father Joe nodded and settled in his favorite recliner. "You came here to kill him," he stated, his tone quiet, unruffled.

Removing his hat, he ran his fingers through his hair then lifted a brow as he eyed Father Joe's untroubled face. "How did you know?" Neither Shawn nor Clayton would have said anything.

"Sit down, Dakota." Father Joe waited until he complied then leaned forward, bracing his arms on his thighs. "Your drive was as obvious as your pain over your mother's death, at least to anyone who cared enough to notice. I worried, but not too much as I've always believed the good in you would overcome the need for revenge. I would watch your face whenever the four of us were together and Shawn or Clayton mentioned their parents' deaths. You admired how they'd handled their losses. Shawn's father was also murdered, but you saw how he accepted the man's prison sentence and moved on. Clayton was as upset as you when he learned the drunk driver who killed his parents was let go on a technicality, but he turned his disappointment into a career of standing up for victims. All along, deep down, you wanted to be as accepting as your friends."

Shaking his head, Dakota had trouble admitting

Father Joe was right. Twenty years of hatred was hard to let go. Then he realized how Poppy had consumed his thoughts more than revenge these past weeks and wondered if it hadn't been for her pushing her way into his life, if he still would have backed off tonight.

"I admit I admire their life choices, but they didn't find their parents' blood-soaked bodies or see who had killed them. But, yeah, there were times I wished I could let my bitterness go. I met someone."

A wide smile blossomed across Father Joe's face. "Ah, that explains a lot. First Shawn, now you. I couldn't be more pleased. We'll have to work on Clayton next."

Dakota snorted. "Good luck with that. I gotta go. My girl needs me." He rose and held out his hand. "Thanks for your input."

"Anytime, son. That's what I'm here for," he said, standing and clasping his hand. "Bring her with you next time and stay longer."

Donning his hat, he nodded and went to the door. "Will do, Father."

CHAPTER ELEVEN

Poppy was emotionally and physically drained by Monday morning, but, as she lay in the hospital bed waiting for the transplant procedure to begin and looked over at her sister, only one thing made her unhappy – how much she wished Dakota were here. After leaving his house last week, she'd flown home with Jerry's blessing and promise to hold her job, and without telling anyone else she was leaving. As grateful as she was for her job, she wasn't sure she would return to Mountain Bend and all the painful memories of losing Dakota.

That hadn't stopped Lisa from calling Jerry when Poppy didn't answer her calls. In the last five days, she'd received well-wishes from half the town of Mountain Bend, the word having traveled fast once she spoke to her friend. If only one of them had been Dakota, she would go into this treatment with enthusiasm instead of a detached apathy she was trying her best to hide.

She'd met her half-sister, Rebecca, the next morning, which perked her up, and her parents couldn't stop smiling as the two of them chatted.

Rebecca didn't hesitate to label their father a self-centered jerk, or say she was sorry she never knew about Poppy until now. According to her, he wasn't interested in digging up the past but offered his support when Rebecca had announced her intentions.

Poppy hadn't, and still didn't care about her sperm donor, but she kept from telling Rebecca that. She understood her sister loved her parents, flaws and all, just as Poppy loved hers. Waving to Rebecca across the room, her sister gave her a thumbs-up in return. She still couldn't believe her luck in finding her, and how enthusiastically Rebecca had jumped in to get tested, saying she'd always wanted a sibling and didn't want to lose her now that they'd found each other. Rebecca's bubbly nature and generosity warmed Poppy, where Dakota's plans had given her cold chills.

During all the final testing and prep for the transplant, which had been minimal since she'd recently gone through this, she'd tried not to dwell on whether he'd gone through with his revenge, and if he were now sitting in jail. If so, there was nothing she could do about it except move on, something she had a lot of experience doing.

Damn, but I really want to hear his voice, see

his scowling face again. She wasn't looking forward to the long road ahead of her, either to recuperate or get over that big, grouchy but lovable jerk.

Her parents entered the pre-op area, her mother carrying a newspaper and wearing a gloating smile. Poppy grinned as they approached, intent on keeping her despondency to herself.

"What is it, Mom? I know that smile, and you're bursting with something that has titillated you."

Her father rolled his eyes and bent to kiss her cheek. "Wait until you hear," he chuckled in her ear.

Opening the paper to the society page, Rose showed her the article on the Mayfields' split, David Mayfield citing irreconcilable differences for filing and sending Constance packing. "She got her just rewards. It seems her husband didn't like the police showing up at their door, questioning them about their employee's actions. The truth came out about her pregnancy, and you, but she swore she knew nothing of Williams' plans."

"I can believe that. She's all about her." Poppy saw her mother's smile dim and concern darken her eyes. Reaching out, she squeezed her arm. "His attempt to get to me failed, thanks to Dakota. That's all that matters."

"That's what I keep telling her." Steve wrapped

an arm around his wife's shoulders and hugged her. "Chin back up. Today is a good day."

"You're right." Rose's smile returned. "You'll have plenty of time to fill us in on this man, Dakota, when you come home to recuperate."

Poppy winced. Been there, done that, and the weeks she'd spent back under her parents' roof recovering from the previous transplant had tested her patience. As much as she adored them, their hovering had driven her crazy.

"I'll come for a week or two. After that, we'll see. The other one took so long because my body fought it. Let's hope my recovery this time is shorter and more successful."

"But—"

"That's a good idea, Poppy," her father interrupted her mother.

Rose opened her mouth to argue, but a commotion at the door drew everyone's attention. Poppy's breath stalled, her pulse skyrocketing when she heard Dakota's belligerent voice demanding to see her.

"I *am* family, damn it. Now, let me in to see her, or call security to try and stop me."

An uncontainable giggle erupted, and Poppy wanted to jump off the bed and run across the room to jump on him. A frustrated, harried-looking nurse headed toward her, but she waved her back. "Let him in," she said, quivering to see him again, praying he hadn't gone through with his revenge.

As soon as he pushed through the door, she went hot, her nipples contracting, her pussy fluttering in response to his arrogant stride, and the scowl darkening his face. Her sister's eyes widened as he went past her then Rebecca sent Poppy another thumbs-up. Dressed in his usual black, shirt sleeves rolled up to his elbows, denim snug enough to showcase his thick thighs, his hat tipped low, shielding those dark eyes she could feel pinning her in place.

"Oh my, Poppy," her mother breathed in awe. "Is that your Dakota?"

"Yes, I am," he said, stopping at Poppy's bedside. Leaning over her, he pinched her chin. "You should have told me about this."

Irked, she narrowed her eyes and returned, "You shouldn't have gone to Phoenix. What happened?" She held her breath, waiting for his answer. When his lips kicked up at the corners, she breathed again.

"Nothing. He's still breathing. For how long is between him and whatever God he believes in, hopefully a vengeful one." Without giving her time to respond, he straightened and turned to her parents, holding out his hand to her father. "Dakota Smith. I'm sorry I'm late to this party. Your daughter neglected to give me a heads-up."

"She can be stubborn," Steve drawled, a twinkle in his eyes. "Steve Flynn, and this is my wife, Rose. Nice to meet you."

"Don't forget me," Rebecca called from the other side of the room, getting chuckles from the two nurses.

Dakota surprised Poppy with his amiable manner as he tipped his hat to her mother, his voice a sexy rumble as he greeted her with a polite, "Ma'am" before strolling over to Rebecca, cupping her face, and planting a kiss on her mouth. "Thank you," he said loud and clear, and Poppy thought her sister would swoon. She didn't know what brought about this change, or what had stopped him from going through with his revenge, but as he came back toward her and her heart skittered, she decided answers could wait.

"We'll let you two visit since they're almost ready for you. We'll be here when you come out." Rose kissed her cheek and whispered in her ear, "I like your young man."

"Me, too."

Her dad winked, and they went to talk to Rebecca. Dakota's phone buzzed as he reached her side again, his scowl returning when he pulled it out. "Shawn again. I swear, I'm going to put Lisa over my lap when we get back for spreading your news around town after pestering Jerry to tell her. Everyone and his brother has been calling."

"I know what you mean." She gave him a teasing grin and whispered, "If you do, I want to watch."

"You would," he retorted then answered the phone. "I just got here, and she'll be going in shortly." He listened a minute then said, "Now that you've asked, yes, there is. Can you and Clayton move her things to my place before we get back?"

Poppy went rigid, and it was her turn to scowl at him when he hung up. "Look, Dakota, just because I love you doesn't mean you can walk all over me, and it especially doesn't mean you can make such decisions without consulting me first." As soon as she stopped talking, she realized what she'd said and clenched her hands under the sheet, waiting for his response, refusing to look away from his unreadable face.

"You see, baby, I disagree, in part." Cupping her nape, he tilted her head and lowered his. "You'll need lots of bedrest to recover, and, in the bedroom,

I have complete control, remember? Just because I love you right back doesn't mean I'll give that up." To prove his point, he took her mouth in a commanding kiss, and Poppy melted inside, her toes curling as the sound of applause rang around the room.

Someone cleared their throat next to her, and, as Dakota released her, she turned to see her doctor smiling. "We're ready for you, if you can pull yourself away from this guy for a short time."

"Go," Dakota insisted. "I'll be here when you get back."

Poppy had never relished anyone's words more than that simple vow, and, as she was wheeled with her new sibling into the treatment room, she was looking forward to staying in one place, with one man, for the first time.

Three months later

Poppy's giggle woke Dakota seconds before two furry bodies crawled up his chest and two wet tongues slimed his face. "Damn it, Poppy. I told you to keep them off the bed." Instead of shooing the puppies away, he rubbed their little shoulders.

"Admit it, you're as ga-ga over the girls as I am."

She pressed her naked body alongside his, and his brain instantly connected with his cock. Poppy's doctors had given her the green light to leave Houston a few weeks ago, her recovery going off without a hitch or any complications. Other than medications to prevent infections and a special diet, she was well on her way back to normal. His patience with her health was a lot better than hers, and they'd butted heads more than once when she tried pushing herself. Luckily, Jerry, along with Miss Betty, were on his side, and Jerry had hired an assistant manager to take on a lot of the physical demands of her job. She'd really been pissed at that, but he had ways of calming her down.

"I wanted one male," he reminded her.

"But they were so cute. Aren't you, sweetie?" She cooed to the dogs, and he gritted his teeth.

"You're ruining them for working."

"Nonsense. They've taken to your training like pros."

When she started in on the baby talk, he snapped, "Cut that out," and lifted the puppies off him and onto the floor then rolled on top of her. "If they piss, you're cleaning it up."

Poppy looped her arms around his neck. "Okay," she agreed without hesitation, nipping his chin. "You're such a grouch in the morning."

"I wouldn't be if you would quit pushing yourself and cheating on your diet."

She nibbled her way down his neck and slid her soft thighs against his legs. "Relax, I won't overdo anything. This isn't my first rodeo, you know. Odds are, given I'm still in remission with no signs of that changing, and this time I had a familial donor, my recovery will be easier and shorter."

"Speaking of Rebecca..." Dakota braced on his right elbow and cupped a breast with his left hand. Her nipple hardened under the stroke of his thumb, her quick responses to his touch never failing to get a stiffer rise out of him. "The spare bedroom is ready whenever she can get away."

"Thanks. I'm looking forward to having her come for a visit. *Dakota.*"

He thought the light glide between her legs would pull a plea from her. Shifting sideways, he stroked his finger downward, grazing her anus as he tugged a nipple with his teeth before saying, "Me, too. I can use the help keeping an eye on you. Clayton's going for the max for Trey Williams." The now ex-employee of the now ex-Mrs. Mayfield pled guilty to an attempted break-in with the intention of doing bodily harm, and Clayton promised to ask for the hard ten.

With a groan, she lifted her pelvis into his hand, whispering, "I figured he would. Clayton mentioned the guy was obsessed with Constance, but she denied there was anything between them."

"It was all one-sided, but that apparently didn't negate the scandal among Houston's elite. Grab hold of the headboard," he instructed as she inched her hand down his chest.

"Fine, but I want my chance."

He slapped her thigh and slid down to wedge his shoulders between her legs. "You don't give the orders here. I don't know why you can't remember that." With deliberate slowness, he licked up her seeping seam then surged upward, bringing her legs over his shoulders with him. "But that's okay. We have a lifetime to work on your obedience."

Poppy's breath caught as he tunneled inside her then she whispered in his ear, "I love you, Master Dakota."

The End

ABOUT BJ WANE

I live in the Midwest with my husband and our Goldendoodle. I love dogs, enjoy spending time with my daughter, grandchildren, reading and working puzzles.

We have traveled extensively throughout the states, Canada and just once overseas, but I now much prefer being homebody.

I worked for a while writing articles for a local magazine but soon found my interest in writing for myself peaking.

My first book was strictly spanking erotica, but I slowly evolved to writing steamy romance with a touch of suspense. My favorite genre to read is suspense.

I love hearing from readers. Feel free to contact me at bjwane@cox.net with questions or comments.

BOOKS BY BJ WANE

VIRGINIA BLUEBLOODS SERIES
Blindsided
Bind Me to You
Surrender to Me
Blackmailed
Bound by Two

MURDER ON MAGNOLIA ISLAND
Logan
Hunter
Ryder

MIAMI MASTERS SERIES
Bound and Saved
Master Me, Please
Mastering Her Fear
Bound to Submit
His to Master and Own
Theirs To Master

COWBOY DOMS SERIES
Submitting to the Rancher
Submitting to the Sheriff
Submitting to the Cowboy
Submitting to the Lawyer
Submitting to Two Doms
Submitting to the Cattleman
Submitting to the Doctor

COWBOY WOLF SERIES
Gavin
Cody
Drake

DOMS OF MOUNTAIN BEND
Protector

SINGLE TITLES
Claiming Mia
Masters of the Castle: Witness Protection Program
Dangerous Interference
Returning to Her Master
Her Master at Last

CONTACT BJ WANE

Website
bjwaneauthor.com

Twitter
twitter.com/bj_wane

Facebook
www.facebook.com/bj.wane
www.facebook.com/BJWaneAuthor

Bookbub
www.bookbub.com/profile/bj-wane

Instagram
www.instagram.com/bjwaneauthor

Goodreads
www.bit.ly/2S6Yg9F